A. A. Dhand was ... watching the city ~~T~~ ... the counter of a small shop. After studying to be a pharmacist, he worked in London and travelled a lot before going back to Bradford to start his own business and begin writing. The history, diversity and darkness of Bradford have inspired his series of novels starring the policeman Harry Virdee.

Darkness Rising

A. A. Dhand

CORGI BOOKS

TRANSWORLD PUBLISHERS
61–63 Uxbridge Road, London W5 5SA
www.penguin.co.uk

Transworld is part of the Penguin Random House group of companies
whose addresses can be found at global.penguinrandomhouse.com

Penguin
Random House
UK

First published in Great Britain in 2020 by Corgi Books
an imprint of Transworld Publishers

A CIP catalogue record for this book
is available from the British Library.

ISBN 9780552177092

Typeset in 12/16pt ITC Stone Serif by Jouve (UK), Milton Keynes
Printed and bound in Great Britain by Clays Ltd, Elcograf S.p.A.

Penguin Random House is committed to a sustainable
future for our business, our readers and our planet. This book
is made from Forest Stewardship Council® certified paper.

MIX
Paper from
responsible sources
FSC® C018179
www.fsc.org

1 3 5 7 9 10 8 6 4 2

For Sam and the boys

Prologue

Zak Choudary was sitting alone by the window inside a late-night kebab shop on Great Horton Road. It was midnight.

Freedom.

After four years of prison.

He was eating a greasy doner kebab. On the house, of course, because Zak was broke. What had his life come to, when he couldn't even afford a shitty takeaway in Bradford? There was nothing worse than being broke. He knew that life. Yet he also knew the other side. Cash was king in Bradford, and dealing drugs had given him plenty of that before he got sent to jail.

Outside, a bright yellow Range Rover stopped in the middle of the road. Behind it came a black Bentley and, behind that, a red Ferrari.

The three drivers got out of their cars, leaving the doors open. They started talking, laughing, joking, shaking hands and slapping each other on the back.

A few cars beeped their horns, but most simply went round them. The drivers were used to this sort of behaviour.

1

These were their streets.

Zak opened his can of coke and took a sip.

Fast cars.

Kings of the city.

He wanted in.

He leaned forwards and saw beautiful white women in the passenger seats of both the Range Rover and the Bentley.

Women, cars and money.

What more did anyone need?

He smiled.

He had never climbed high enough to reach that level. But still, Zak knew what a five-grand heap of cash felt like in his hands. He missed the sight of a ten-grand Rolex on his wrist, and the excitement of escorts and hotel rooms. Prison had taken all that from him. He certainly couldn't survive on the government benefits he was getting now. He knew what he needed to do.

The kebab house was busy with young lads. Almost all of them were watching the display outside, seduced by the lifestyle.

That is what this was.

Seduction of the young.

The blonde in the Range Rover got out of the car, her dress tight, showing enough skin to ensure everyone looked at her.

She walked down to the Bentley, leaned over

brazenly and spoke to the other woman through the passenger window.

The lads in the shop started to jeer and whoop.

Zak smiled.

This was Bradford.

This was power.

His phone beeped.

Upstairs.

From the first-floor window, Zak had an even better view of the cars and the women outside.

'Exciting, isn't it?' said a voice from behind him.

A voice he knew. A voice that held the real power. A senior member of the West-side drug gang, currently fighting for territory with Bradford-East.

'It is,' said Zak. He could not hide the longing in his voice.

'Do you remember that life?'

'I never climbed that high.'

'You want to?'

Zak turned round. 'Does a man who pops Viagra want to fuck?'

The man laughed. 'When was the last time you got laid?'

'Yesterday.'

'Emily?'

Zak nodded.

3

'At £150 a time, she is not bad. Not quite the level you're looking at out there, though,' said the man.

Zak desperately wanted that life. 'I have been in jail for four years. Emily is more than enough.'

'Do you like her? Want her to be a long-term fixture?'

Zak put his hands in his pockets. 'Nothing is for free in this world. Drugs, women or favours.'

The man stayed where he was, hidden in the shadows. He spoke quietly of a big police action the previous year. The raid had resulted in dozens of gang members going to jail. That had hurt their empire. It gave the East-side gangs the chance for more power. What the West-side needed now was muscle. Someone to put fear on the streets. Someone who could take a life without thinking. This would send a message across the city that the West-side gang was no longer weak.

'Can you be that man, Zak?'

'You know I can. Lives have a price. Power doesn't.'

The man laughed. 'Same old Zak. Tell me, how much money do you have in your pocket right now?'

Zak didn't answer.

'That bad, huh? And what were you clearing before prison? Two grand a week?'

Zak nodded. He hated being penniless. When he spoke this time, his voice carried real purpose. 'I want to climb the ranks. Earn what those boys outside are getting.'

The man came out from the shadows.

A face Zak had not seen for years.

'To do that, Zak, first you need to be feared. The money comes along with that. Show the streets who controls them.'

'I can do that.'

'Then, Zak Choudary, you and I are going to do just fine. There's work to be done. People to be taken care of.'

The man put his arm round Zak. He pointed towards the cars outside, still blocking traffic.

'You give me a year, Zak Choudary, and I will give you the streets. He who controls the streets, controls Bradford. Once you have that, you will never have to worry about money again.'

Chapter One

Detective Inspector Harry Virdee finished his morning run around Lister Park and began the walk home to his house on Oak Lane. His phone showed a message from his wife.

No shampoo left! How is a pregnant woman supposed to wash her bloody hair! Get some from the corner shop or I will end you, Hardeep Virdee!

Hardeep.

She only called him by his full name when she was pissed off.

The text was ten minutes old.

Harry quickened his pace.

In the hallway, Harry paused by a small table. An old pair of slippers was resting on top. He touched them, then his own head.

The slippers were Harry's mother, Joyti's. She had given them to him three years before, when he married Saima. Harry was Sikh, his wife was Muslim, and the marriage had cost him everything. His father, Ranjit, had come at him with his kirpan, the dagger carried by many devout Sikhs, intending to kill him. Joyti had finally

7

stepped in and led Harry outside. Before closing the door, she had taken off her slippers.

'My boy, you have touched my feet every morning since I can remember. But now, this home is not yours any more. No longer will my feet be here for you to touch. No more will I be able to bless you. Take these instead.'

Upstairs, Harry entered the bathroom, which was now full of steam.

'How long have you been in here?' asked Harry, blinking hard as the steam hit his eyes. He could barely see Saima.

'You can run miles around that park, yet when I need shampoo it takes you how long?'

'I only got your text ten minutes ago.'

'Liar.'

Harry started to undress, hoping Saima had not used up all the hot water.

'Actually, you're right, I did get distracted. There was this sexy white chick who had a flat tyre. I helped her change it.'

The shower stopped. Saima stuck her head out from behind the curtain. 'Two things. One, winding up a pregnant woman is likely to get you killed. And two, this pregnant woman also happens to be a senior A&E nurse. I could stab you, make the bleeding last and prolong the pain of death.'

'I love it when you talk dirty.'

'Piss off. Where's my shampoo?'

Harry handed her the bottle.

Saima frowned. 'What is this?'

'They were out of Head and Shoulders. It was this or nothing.'

'69p? Really?'

'Two for a pound but there was only one left.'

'Did you tell the shop owner you would come back for it later?'

Harry grabbed her face and kissed her forehead. 'You are the stingiest woman I've ever met.'

'A bargain is a bargain. I will be in that shop later.'

Saima's head dipped behind the curtain. The water was turned back on.

Harry finished undressing.

'Can I get in there with you? If you breathe in, I might fit.'

Saima's face reappeared. 'You think you're funny, don't you?'

Harry nodded.

'Hot water is finished,' she said, smiling wickedly.

Harry sighed and helped her step out of the tub.

'Karma is a bitch,' said Saima, and blew him a kiss.

After a brisk, cold shower, Harry was in the kitchen. He stared at the baby name chart on the fridge. There were two columns – one for Harry and one for Saima. Across the top of the chart was a highlighted note.

'No *peeps*. No *deeps*. No *eenas*.'

They were trying to find the perfect name for their little girl. *Peeps* and *deeps* meant traditional Sikh names. On Harry's side of the chart, those names had been crossed through – Jasdeep, Ramandeep, Sharandeep. He didn't like those names either. He had put them there to make a point.

Eenas were more Muslim-sounding names – Aleena, Shameena, Rabeena.

They needed a blend. To date, they had nothing.

Harry looked at the chart and saw two new additions. Rukhsana and Aiyla.

He put a cross through both of them. 'Nice try,' he whispered.

There was also a message scrawled in large block capitals. *WEDDING RECEPTION TONIGHT. WE ARE GOING! NO EXCUSES!*

Harry sighed. He hated Asian wedding par-
ties, full of over-the-top celebrations.

He had just put the kettle on when his phone
started to ring.

'Boss?' It was Detective Sergeant Simon Palmer,
Harry's colleague. 'We've got another body.'

Chapter Two

Harry was crouched by the victim, in an old cobbled alley off Water Lane. Ahead was the Crabtree Mill, one of many abandoned mills in the city. At one point Bradford had been one of the richest cities in Europe, with a thriving textile trade. Those times were long gone.

Harry winced at the needles sticking out of the dead man's eyeballs. The cause of death was clearly the gunshot wound to the guy's chest, a hole the size of a tennis ball. So why the needles?

Damn city was dropping more bodies than anywhere else in the north of England.

Heroin was the problem. It flooded into the city. Everyone it touched was sentenced to a lifetime of misery, or else death in the streets.

A cordon had been set up by uniformed police. Crime-scene investigators swarmed over the area.

'Needles again, eh?' said DS Simon Palmer, arriving by Harry's side.

Harry got to his feet, allowing the police photographer to start snapping pictures of the victim.

'This city is never going to change,' said Harry, sighing.

'This is the second one. One more and we will be looking for a serial killer,' said Palmer, nodding at the addict's eyes.

'Same calling card doesn't mean same killer,' replied Harry. Bradford had had several serial killers in its history. It damn well didn't need another.

The first victim had been found two weeks before. A well-known drug-dealer, he too had been found outside an empty mill with needles sticking out of his eyes. Both victims also had their mouths full of a brownish powder.

Street heroin.

Harry didn't want to admit it, but this almost certainly was the same killer.

This victim was Asian, male and probably in his late thirties. He had no flesh on him. Hundreds of needle marks pierced his body.

'Looks like a message from one drug gang to another – keep off our turf,' said Harry.

'Similar to the last victim, boss. No CCTV in the area.'

Harry glanced around. 'These dealers know the blind spots in this city.'

'The East-side, West-side drug war continues,' said Palmer.

Harry rubbed a tired hand across his face. Sleeping next to Saima when she was so heavily pregnant was difficult. He could not remember the last time he had slept through the night.

'Until one gang takes out the other, nothing will change. Nobody is going to talk. Simpson is going to be pissed off.'

Detective Superintendent George Simpson was their boss. With a fortnight to go before his retirement, he was going to be fuming that there was another murder while he was in charge.

Harry asked about the rest of his team. Palmer told him four of them were off sick.

'Four?' said Harry, displeased.

'Norovirus. One got it. Passed it down the line. They are all at home with diarrhoea. To be honest, boss, I'm not feeling too good myself.'

Harry joked. 'Simon, if you get the runs, I am going to kick you up the arse so hard you will never take a decent shit again.'

'Thanks, boss. I'm feeling better already.'

Their team had been ruined by government cuts. They had lost nearly a quarter of the staff. Now, with the rest out sick, Harry was going to have to work this alone. Palmer would man the office. They needed to find the killer before this war grew bigger.

Harry stepped back and took in the scene,

hands in his pockets, his breath forming a white mist in the icy breeze. This part of the city was known for two things – drugs and poverty, which meant the locals were often known to the police. Harry stared up at the ghostly Crabtree building and saw a shadow move away from a broken window.

'Back in a minute, Simon.'

Harry forced the rear entrance open. It took little effort – the wooden door was rotten. He stepped into a dark and decaying space. He had left DS Palmer controlling the scene outside. Palmer was a straight-shooter, he played by the rules.

Harry was different.

He moved slowly up the cold staircases that snaked around the building, keeping away from discarded syringes and used condoms. His shoes crunched on broken glass. Graffiti was scrawled across every wall.

On the top floor, Harry paused outside some flimsy wooden doors and listened.

Nothing.

Harry opened the doors and stepped inside. The smell of decay and damp hit him immediately.

He stopped in the centre of the room, taking in every corner, seeing nothing but shadows.

'It's minus two out there today. Twenty quid gets you a few hot meals,' he called out.

Nothing.

He walked to the far window, which had broken glass around its edges. From here he could see the crime scene, the body still on the floor. A nearby street light would have given a clear view, even late at night.

Harry stayed where he was, but turned round and spoke to the shadows again.

'Maybe hot meals aren't what you need. Maybe it's a couple of heroin wraps. Not my business how you spend the money.'

There was movement in the far corner. Slowly, the outline of a woman came into view. She was thin, her hair hanging across her face. She wore a loose T-shirt and ripped jeans. She must have been freezing.

Harry kept his hands in his pockets and carefully moved towards her.

'I'm Detective Inspector Harry Virdee. I'm with the Bradford Homicide and Major Enquiry Team. And you are?'

The girl didn't answer.

Harry took a hand from one pocket, clutching a twenty-pound note.

'Shelley.'

'You stay here a lot, Shelley?'

She nodded, keeping her eyes on the money.

'Someone was murdered outside here last night. You might know something about it.'

She shrugged. 'Lot of things happen outside them windows.'

'No doubt. It's Bradford, after all. Wouldn't be home if nothing happened.'

Harry smiled and the girl did the same.

'You know the second-hand clothes shop on Great Horton?'

The girl nodded.

'Ask for Farhana. Tell her that Harry said to give you some warm clothes. She's a good woman. She will sort you out.'

'And for that you want what? Me on my knees?'

'No. Even if we can't help each other right now, the clothes are yours. This city takes people one of two ways. The drugs I can't help with. The cold I can.'

She smiled again. 'What are you? Some sort of Robin Hood?'

Harry thought about his unborn daughter. If this was her, he hoped someone would do the same thing.

'I care about my city, about its people. It's why I became a cop.'

She shrugged. 'I seen what happened last night.'

He waited but she didn't say any more.

17

'Why don't we go and get breakfast? There's a new cafe in North Parade – Bread and Roses. Hot coffee, bagels with melted butter and the best carrot cake in this city. You fancy it?'

She licked her lips without thinking, and then said, 'Did you find needles in the guy's eyes?'

Harry stepped closer to her. She couldn't have seen that level of detail from this high up. That meant only one thing – she knew who did this.

Harry waved the twenty-pound note at her. 'Shelley, let's go get that breakfast.'

Chapter Three

Harry ordered them each a hot breakfast and coffee. They ate in silence. Harry noticed how quickly Shelley ate her meal. She had finished before he had even eaten half of his.

'So, what do you know?' Harry asked her.

'I heard that girls like me can get paid regular for helping the police.'

Harry sipped his coffee and nodded. 'Sometimes.'

'I reckon I can tell you stuff about Bradford you don't know.'

'How about we start with last night? If your information works out, I will see what we can sort out.'

Harry took the twenty-pound note from his pocket and put it on the table. Shelley moved to take it and he put his palm over it.

'If it works out – it's yours.'

She took her hand back and wrapped it round her mug of coffee.

'Start from the beginning,' he said.

Shelley paused, as if thinking about how much to tell Harry.

'About a year ago,' she said, 'you guys took down a big part of the West-side drug gang. Like, twenty people or something?'

Harry nodded. One of the biggest drugs busts in England.

'Well, you jailed most of the really bad guys, the ones who scare people into doing what the bosses want. The East-side gang started moving in, taking up territory. Things got messy.'

'There's always a turf war going on in this city,' said Harry. He could not see where this was going.

'A few months back, this guy gets out of prison. Small-time player in the West-side gang when he went inside. Now, though, he sees an opportunity. New muscle. If you control the streets, you control the supply. If you control the supply, you control the money. And once you have that . . . you have the girls.'

Harry sipped his coffee. She was scared of this guy, he could tell.

'The needles?' he prompted.

'I heard it's his thing. He puts them in your eyes, lets you suffer and then he kills you. It's all about a reputation. And it's working. Nobody will speak out against him.'

'Give me a name, Shelley.'

'Zak Choudary. You know him?'

Harry shook his head.

'Thought you were a detective.'

'Murder police. Not drugs.'

'Same thing around here, isn't it?'

Harry nodded. It was true.

'I saw Zak last night, outside the mill. There was a fight.'

Harry pushed his coffee aside, no longer wanting it. He needed to know if she was telling him the truth. 'It's a fair distance from the top of the Crabtree Mill to the side of Water Lane where we found the body.'

Shelley smiled. 'I've seen him a lot.'

'Is he a . . . client?' he asked, taking a punt.

She laughed. 'Client? He likes a higher class of girl. My . . . sister, Emily. She's, you know, the classy sort.'

'You mean an escort?'

She nodded and stopped talking, looking instead at the money on the table. Harry slid it over towards her and watched her stuff it in her coat pocket.

'I wasn't always like this. I used to be that higher class of girl. Emily and I got in with the wrong crowd. Me with the worst. At least she isn't a slave to the needle, turning tricks for ten quid a time.'

Harry stared at her, trying to see the woman she used to be.

'You don't believe me?'

'I do. This city can be cruel.'

'I had dreams, you know. Community college. Hairdressing, beauty. All of that. Bad crowd, bad fella . . . bad times.'

Harry leaned forward and lowered his voice. 'I would like to meet this guy. Zak.'

Shelley sat back in her chair and ran her hand through dirty blonde hair.

'My sister's in trouble. She's Zak's girl.'

'Girl?'

'The bosses keep girls on their payroll. Especially for those just out of prison, to keep them happy. Exclusive, just for them. They all get possessive. But Emily told me she's frightened of Zak. He can be, you know – a bit . . . rough. She doesn't know what to do. I might be a mess, Harry, but she's still my little sister and I want to help her.'

'Let me do that, then.'

'You're a police officer with a set of handcuffs and loads of rules and regulations.'

Harry shrugged. 'I guess I will have to leave my badge in my pocket then. Do you know where I can find him?'

She shook her head. 'He's not that stupid. No one knows where he is. He comes to you.'

'And Emily?'

'He goes to her. Whenever he pleases. I can give you the next best thing, though.'

Harry waited for more. Shelley pulled the money from her pocket and waved it at him. 'Doesn't stretch that far.'

'If you help me, I will make sure there is more where that came from.'

'Zak has a blue-script at Rimmington Pharmacy.'

Harry knew the term. A blue-script was a daily prescription for a methadone treatment programme. Drug-addicts were enrolled when released from prison.

'How do you know?'

'It's where I go to get mine.'

Harry took a pad from his pocket and made a note. He needed one last thing, though. Harry put his hand over Shelley's.

'You can trust me, I promise you.'

'What more do you need?'

'I need to speak to Emily.'

Chapter Four

Harry put a call in to DS Palmer. He told him to find all he could about Zak Choudary – his prison record, probation details, anything.

He left Kirkgate and drove towards the Lister Mills complex, a swanky new apartment building.

Shelley had called Emily to confirm she was home, but had not told her about Harry. Emily wouldn't have agreed to meet him.

Harry used Shelley's key-code to get into the lifts and up to the top floor.

He rang the doorbell and waited. He heard footsteps behind the door and then a female voice asked who was there.

Harry wanted to be discreet. The last thing he wanted was for Emily to get into trouble. He took a business card and pen from his pocket and scribbled on the back.

Shelley sent me. I would rather not announce to the whole corridor who I am . . .

Harry slipped the card underneath the door.

A few minutes later, the door opened.

*

Harry watched Emily making coffee. She had reached into a cupboard, which he had seen was empty.

'My sister talks too much,' she said, without turning round. Harry didn't detect any annoyance in her voice. In fact, quite the opposite.

She brought the drinks over and set them down on the table. Before she could sit down, Harry put his hand out.

'One thing,' he said.

She paused. 'Yes?'

'That tiny dot on top of the empty cupboard. A camera, no? Turn it off, will you? I'm not a punter. You're not in danger.'

She looked at him, aghast.

'It's smart, recording what happens when you're working. Well, before you became exclusively Zak's girl, right?'

Emily didn't reply.

'This, though, isn't work,' said Harry.

Emily walked back to the cabinet and turned off the camera.

It was a tiny, portable device.

'Could you bring it over here please?' said Harry.

She did so.

Harry checked it was indeed off. He stuffed it into the couch.

'What do you want?' said Emily.

'Zak Choudary.'

She shrugged. 'So, go and arrest him.'

'If I knew where he was, I might.'

'Might?'

Harry didn't want to tell her that he didn't have enough evidence to arrest Zak yet. Shelley had been firm – she was not snitching. Harry would have to try to get someone else to go on record. To do that, he needed to get closer to Zak's inner circle.

'Just tell me how you know Zak.'

Emily confirmed what Shelley had already told him, that she was Zak's private escort, paid for by people higher up. She didn't say who. She probably didn't know. Harry didn't ask. The deal would have been sorted by low-level players, errand boys.

'Are you happy with this set-up?'

'It's fine.'

Her tone said otherwise.

'Doesn't sound it.'

'I'm on payroll. It's stable, steady, no hassle.'

'How long has it been . . . a thing?'

'Few months.'

She couldn't look at Harry.

Harry studied her more closely.

Polo-neck jumper. Black jeans, sleeves pulled over her hands.

She had bruises to cover.

Shelley had been right to send him here.

'I've heard Zak can be a little ... heavy-handed.'

She said nothing.

Harry stood up. 'Emily, would you mind standing up, please?'

She stayed seated.

'Come on,' he said, offering his hand.

She ignored it and got to her feet.

'Turn round please.'

Harry could see that she knew what was coming.

'Could you raise your jumper for me please?'

Emily dropped her head on to her chest. She didn't refuse. This confirmed what Harry had suspected – that she wanted help. Slowly, she raised her jumper.

Harry winced.

Emily started to cry.

Chapter Five

At Trafalgar House, police headquarters, Harry told DS Palmer what had happened.

'But neither girl will come forward?' Palmer asked.

'No, we need something else.'

Palmer had information from the Police National-al Database, drug and alcohol services and the probation teams. Before prison, Zak Choudary had been a low-level member of the West-side drug gang. Four years ago, aged twenty-seven, he had been given an eight-year prison sentence for dealing drugs. Now he was out on parole.

Zak had many cautions for affray and assault going back to his teenage years. His descent into Bradford's drug-fuelled streets was clear for Harry to see. Minor crimes, street fights, drugs, then prison. When Zak had been arrested, he had heroin and over eight thousand pounds in cash on him. To come out of prison and look for a steady job was very hard. Once you got used to earning that kind of cash, working for mini-mum wage was difficult to accept.

His records had him listed as NFA – no fixed

abode – although there was a name, Natalie Zurek, and an address. Palmer believed her to be an ex-girlfriend.

'I will see what Natalie's got to say once I've been to the pharmacy,' Harry said. 'Palmer, I need you to work out what connects our two victims. We know it's drugs but I need something solid.'

'Looks like it's going to be a late one, boss.'

Harry looked around at the empty desks. 'Not for me. Got to take Saima to a wedding reception tonight. I've already been warned not to be late.'

'Rather you than me.'

Harry left his desk and headed towards his boss's office.

'Palmer briefed me about the body this morning,' said DSU George Simpson, shaking his head.

'I'm pretty sure it's drug-related, sir.'

'Sounds it.'

Simpson got up from his chair and walked over to Harry. He lifted a wooden chair, put it by Harry, and sat down.

'You're a good detective, Harry.'

'Thank you, sir.'

'Not afraid to walk that fine line between law and disorder.'

Harry smiled. 'I don't know what you mean.'

Simpson put his hand on Harry's shoulder. 'I'm out of here in a fortnight. Can't say I will miss the place.'

'Don't I know it, sir.'

'Two dead dealers, killed in similar ways. Only a matter of time before the other side replies. And in this city, that can lead to all kinds of problems. I would rather retire on a positive note.'

'I'm on it, sir.'

'You bring this home quickly and quietly, Harry, and I will owe you.'

Chapter Six

Harry approached Rimmington Pharmacy.

This part of town was lively, but it hadn't always been. The city centre had been flattened a decade ago, ready to be rebuilt. Then the recession happened and the rebuilding was put on hold. For years the site had been known as the 'hole in the ground'. Thankfully, times were changing. Shops, cafes, gyms and restaurants were opening up, and a new Westfield shopping centre was breathing life into the area.

An assistant wearing a name badge, which said *Laura*, greeted Harry politely.

'Can I help you?'

Harry placed his police identification on the counter. 'I need a word with the pharmacist.'

The girl looked at his badge then moved to the back of the store where a young Asian woman in a headscarf had her head down, no doubt checking medications. Harry saw a notice on the side of the counter that said, *Responsible pharmacist – Aneela Baig*.

Laura returned and said, 'She's checking a few prescriptions. If you can wait a few minutes?'

'Sure.'

'There's a consultation room just over there. Would you like to wait inside?'

The private consultation room was tiny, with healthcare notices all over the walls. Harry sat down and read a few – hepatitis, HIV, clean needles, helplines.

The door opened and Aneela entered. She was a tiny woman, barely five foot tall. Harry stood up and introduced himself. They both sat down.

'I understand you treat a methadone addict here called Zak Choudary.'

Her face gave nothing away.

'Well, do you?'

'What is this in regards to, please?'

'Does he come here or not?'

'I cannot breach patient confidentiality.'

'You're seriously going to play that card?'

She shrugged. 'It's not a card, Detective, it's the law.'

Harry leaned a little closer. 'I'm well aware of the law, Ms Baig.'

'Then you will know you need the appropriate paperwork.'

The thing Harry hated most – someone who sticks to the rules, a jobsworth.

He sighed and leaned back in his chair. 'Do you own this place?'

She nodded.

'How many addicts do you have on the books? Can you tell me that much? Not breaking any rules there, are we?'

She thought about it. 'Fifty-nine.'

Harry whistled. 'That's a lot of methadone.'

'It is.'

'Correct me if I'm wrong but you get paid for that, right? Each time you hand it out?'

'We get paid to oversee their doses.'

'How much?'

Aneela frowned. 'Why?'

'I'm interested.'

She shrugged.

Harry allowed the silence to linger, until she looked away.

'Tell you what, Aneela,' he said, standing up. 'I will place myself outside your front door and ask every addict who turns up whether he knows Zak Choudary. A copper standing outside your pharmacy, hassling addicts? That can't be good for business. Maybe I will come back tomorrow and the day after that until I get some answers. If I was an addict, I would be looking for another pharmacy.'

She stared at him, in shock.

Harry sat down again. 'Thing is, Aneela, I've been where you are. Owning a little business. My dad had a corner shop, and customers are king, right? Last thing I want to do is be a headache. You and I have better things to do. All I'm looking for is a professional favour on a serious matter. I work in homicide and I've got a killer who might strike again.'

'He . . . er . . . usually comes in first thing in the mornings with another addict.'

'Usually?'

'This morning he arrived alone. He had a new prescription and he's now on two-day supplies. He won't be back here until the day after tomorrow.'

'The other guy, his mate, hasn't collected yet today?'

She shook her head.

'Do you have an address for Zak?'

'No fixed abode. Most of the methadone programme are NFA.'

'What about his mate, the one who's usually with him. What's he called?'

'Dennis McTurk.'

'Address?'

She looked at him, raised her eyebrows.

Also NFA, then.

34

'What does he look like?'

'You can't miss him. He's got bright orange hair – dyed. In a Mohawk. Pretty striking.'

Harry scribbled his mobile number in his notebook, tore off the page and handed it to her. 'When Dennis comes today, how long can you delay him?'

'Not long. We measure the methadone the night before. It is all ready for when they arrive.'

'Can you tell him you're in short supply and to call back later? At a given time so I can collar him?'

'Not a chance. He will kick off. When they need their methadone, that is all that matters.'

Harry nodded. 'I understand. Will you at least call me and let me know?'

'I've already been more than helpful, Mr Virdee.' Aneela stood and reached for the door.

Harry was sitting on a bench by the pharmacy thinking about his next move when he saw what had to be Dennis McTurk with his orange Mohawk walking towards him. Harry got to his feet.

'Dennis?'

'Who's asking?' replied the man, swallowing the last of a can of Skol Super extra-strength lager. He crumpled the can in his hands.

'I'm Detective Harry Virdee of the Major Homicide and Enquiry Team—'

Harry got no further. Dennis threw the empty beer can at him and made a break for it, running wildly back the way he had come.

Harry went after him.

Chapter Seven

They were running towards the top of town, uphill.

Harry eased up. Dennis was slowing, the hill getting steeper. Another few yards and it was over. Dennis slumped on to a bench, wheezing.

Harry grabbed his shoulder and hauled him to his feet, pulling him into a small cobbled side-street.

McTurk tried to lash out with a punch, but Harry caught his fist. Then Harry grabbed him by the throat and said, 'Don't be a damn fool.'

He let go and waited for McTurk to sit down.

Instead, he keeled over and vomited all over the floor.

'Jesus,' said Harry, moving away.

He waited till McTurk had finished, folded his arms across his chest and said, 'Well?'

McTurk wiped his mouth, smearing vomit across his sleeve.

Harry winced. He didn't want to get too close.

'Well, what? Fucking harassment is what this is. I did nuffink. You pigs all the same.'

'Just wanted a chat.'

'About what?'

'Zak Choudary.'

'Never heard of him.'

Harry reached down and slapped the side of McTurk's head. He stared up at Harry, stunned.

'I can't do that. Right?' said Harry.

McTurk said nothing.

'Thing is, I'm a different kind of cop. All that form-filling and policy and rules isn't my thing. You want to file a complaint about me, that's just fine. My word against yours.' Harry stepped a little closer, his voice quieter now. 'Who are people going to believe? You? Or me? All I'm looking for is a little information on Zak. After that we don't ever need to meet again.' Harry pointed back the way they had come. 'Or I nick you for attempted assault, which means you might not get your methadone today.'

McTurk simply nodded.

'Turn your pockets out,' said Harry.

'Why?'

The change in McTurk was swift. He had something to hide. Harry had seen this hundreds of times before.

'I want to know what you've got to hide.'

'You got no right!'

'We've been over that. Empty your pockets or I will do it for you.'

McTurk glanced around but they were alone. There was no help coming his way. Reluctantly, he emptied his pockets and threw the contents on the floor.

Cigarettes, a lighter, some receipts and a woolly hat.

'That it?'

McTurk nodded.

Harry smiled. 'I'm not buying it.'

'I got nuffink!'

Harry waited.

Slowly, McTurk produced four £10 heroin wraps and threw them on the ground. 'They ain't mine. I was holding them for someone!'

McTurk's hand still rested by his pocket.

Harry waited.

'Five seconds then I pat you down.'

McTurk cursed and took a heavy-looking bag of brown powder from his pocket. He dropped it on the ground, away from where he had vomited, and put his head in his hands.

Harry whistled. Looked like half a kilo, easy. He picked up the bag.

'You must be the dumbest dealer I've ever seen, walking around with this in your pocket.'

'I found it. On my way to the pharmacy.'

'Of course you did. How long have you been out?'

McTurk didn't answer.

'Still on parole?'

Again he stayed silent.

Harry laughed. 'Oh, you are fully fucked now, aren't you, boy?'

Harry put the drugs in his pocket.

'I need that. I'm dead without it.'

'You need to worry about me, first. Zak – what can you tell me about him?'

'Nuffink! I known him like a month, man.'

'Enough time. Where does he live? What does he do?'

McTurk shrugged. 'He was at that prisoner-release hostel with me and then he found some place.'

'Some place?'

'Family or somefink.'

'Where?'

'I don't know. Honest.'

Harry picked up one of the wraps. He opened it and dumped the heroin on the ground, on top of the vomit.

'Shit! No! I got to pay for that.'

'I know.'

Harry started on another wrap. It sent McTurk crazy. He got up, waved his hands furiously at Harry and stamped his feet on the ground. 'This is bullshit!'

Harry was unfazed. 'You better give me some-thing useful.'

McTurk was desperate. 'There's this place – a shisha bar. Down Thornton Road. Said he got connections there.'

Harry knew the place.

McTurk eyed the heroin wraps greedily.

'Whose are these?' asked Harry.

'Huh?'

'Which dealer?'

McTurk looked away.

'You were doing so well there, Dennis.'

'Like I said, I found them.'

'Two things are going to happen now, Den-nis. First, I'm going to check out what you told me about the shisha bar. It had better pan out. Second, if Zak gets in touch, I expect a call. And for that, I might think about giving you your drugs back.'

McTurk looked at him, clearly unsure.

'I'm murder police,' said Harry. 'I'm not fuck-ing around for a bag of heroin. Told you, I'm about getting shit done.'

Chapter Eight

Harry walked up the drive at Natalie Zurek's house, past a battered old Ford Focus.

If Natalie was involved in the drug trade, wouldn't she have a flashier vehicle?

Harry rang the doorbell and waited. Inside, he could hear a child crying – in full-on meltdown mode.

'Who is it?' came a shrill female voice.

He heard her curse when he shouted his name.

'Can you come back another time please?'

'No, I'm afraid not,' said Harry.

The door flew open and he came face-to-face with a young brunette, face flushed. A child continued to cry from inside the house.

'What is it?' she said.

'I need to speak to you about Zak Choudary.'

'I got nothing to do with him any more.'

'Really? Because, on his release from prison, he listed this address as where he was staying.'

She sighed, stepped aside and said, 'You can have five minutes.'

*

Harry sat alone in the living room. Next door, in the kitchen, Natalie tried to calm her five-year-old son, Jack. Harry thought of Saima, home alone, heavily pregnant. They had all this to look forward to. Today could be the day. And they still didn't have a name.

Harry fired Saima a text.

Zara?

She replied immediately. *Yes! Love it!*

Harry frowned. That was a first.

He Googled the origins of the name, saw that it was also an Islamic name and replied, *Veto. Islamic origins.*

You shit! she replied.

Harry put his phone away.

Natalie had calmed Jack down and returned to the living room without him.

'This needs to be quick,' she said, sitting opposite Harry.

'How long have you lived here?'

'A year.'

'When was the last time you saw Zak Choudary?'

'Four years ago, when he went to jail.'

'Really?'

'Really.'

'Spoken to him since then?'

'No.'

43

Harry smiled. 'Really upsets me when bad liars don't think about what they are saying.'

'I'm not lying.'

'You are.'

She said nothing.

'He went to jail four years ago. You haven't spoken to or seen him since. Yet he knows where you live, and you only moved here a year ago.'

She closed her eyes and sighed. 'Shit.'

Harry leaned forward. 'Now we're in trouble because we have lost the trust part of this chat.'

When she opened her eyes, they were filled with tears. She chewed her lip, glanced behind her to where Jack was playing in the next room.

'Do you have children?' she asked, turning to face him.

'Expecting my first. Due any day.'

'Your life will change. You have no idea.'

'I'm sure,' said Harry. 'That's Zak's kid, isn't it?'

She nodded.

'Does he know?'

Another nod.

She was afraid. It was all over her face. He thought of Emily and the bruises. This guy was turning out to be quite something. Everyone was afraid of him.

44

'I can make things safe for you.'

She laughed. 'God, you are so out of touch. Are you new to Bradford or something?'

That hurt Harry.

'The police don't run this city, or protect it, any more. Dealers do. They drive around in 100K Range Rovers and pay no taxes. They wear 20K Rolex watches, and claim Universal Credit. Then you rock up here, telling me you can make me safe?'

Everything she had said was true. Every night, driving down Leeds Road, you could see the show of power from people who had no right to any. It was an insult.

'When did you last see him?'

She didn't reply.

'Look, we can do this here or I can drag you down to the station and make a real show of it.'

She stared at him. 'Why do you want to know about him anyway?'

'Enquiries.'

'About?'

Harry was going to say *Murder*, but he didn't want to scare her.

'Criminal activity.'

She shrugged. 'Dealers deal.'

Harry waited for more, fixing her with a hard stare. Jack was singing in the background now.

'Listen to your boy. Happy. Carefree. Let's keep it that way. All I want is Zak.'

She put her head in her hands and took a moment before speaking.

'He called me from prison a few months ago. Said he was coming out. Said he wanted to see Jack. That he had rights.'

She didn't look at Harry, keeping her head in her hands.

'I didn't want a court battle. I don't have the money. So I said he could see Jack once a month until he had proved he had changed. He asked if he could use my address, say he was living with me, and I agreed. Seemed harmless.'

She looked at Harry now. 'Harmless. More fool me, huh.'

There was more. Harry could see it.

'Tell me,' he said. 'I promise you, I can help. If I give you my word that I can keep you safe, I mean it.'

Harry saw that she wanted to believe him.

Natalie swallowed hard.

'Did Zak . . . hurt you?'

Her look said it all.

Harry clenched his teeth.

'I just wanted to keep Jack safe. He didn't, you know, force me. I just . . . let it happen.'

Harry got up and sat next to her.

'Natalie, I want this bastard to go away. And I can make that happen. I promise you.'

Harry needed her to confirm that Zak had re-entered Bradford's evil drug-trade. He needed to check the information he had been given by Shelley and her sister. The family tie between Emily and Shelley meant they might have been working together for their own reasons. But Harry needed to be sure that he wasn't being conned.

A quarter-hour later, Harry had the information he needed.

Chapter Nine

Thornton Road was the old red-light district of Bradford. In recent years it had changed, mostly because of the new student housing, built for the nearby university.

Harry felt uneasy about how he had left things with Natalie. The last thing she wanted was to be involved with whatever Zak was doing. She could lose custody of her child. Harry had offered to place panic alarms in her home, connected to the police. She had been horrified. Zak turned up when he wanted – there was no pattern.

Harry had left his mobile number with her, the only thing he could really do.

He stopped his car outside Arabian Delightz, the shisha bar Dennis McTurk had told him about. This place was well known to Harry. An obvious, almost brazen drug den, it was where all the dealers came to hang out. There were never any drugs inside. It was just a protected space where they could talk business and relax. Security was tight. Only members were let in.

If what McTurk had said turned out to be true and Zak Choudary was a member of this place, it meant only one thing – he really had risen up the ranks since he left prison.

The sign for Arabian Delightz was bright neon green. Harry parked in a side-street, working through all the set-ups he was likely to meet inside. He needed to speak with Zak Choudary. If Harry had evidence or witnesses, he would have arrived with a warrant and back-up police. But he had nothing.

The club was a no-go area for police officers. He would not be welcome, but Harry wasn't afraid of that.

The entrance was guarded by a bouncer. Harry tried to step past him but a solid hand was placed on his chest.

'Members only, Brother.'

'What's your name?'

'People just call me Sheikh.'

Harry took a step back. 'I'm here on business,' he said, showing Sheikh his ID. 'Step aside.'

Harry again tried to pass him, and again felt a firm hand on his chest.

'Do you have a warrant? If not, I suggest you go and get one.'

'What if I don't want to get one? What if I want to step inside? Have a look around.'

The hand remained on Harry's chest. He looked at it. Then at Sheikh.

'You put your hand on me again, it's assault.'
Harry took a pair of handcuffs from his pocket.
'Your choice. Either move or be moved.'

Sheikh looked uncertain. Harry presumed it
had been a while since he had been challenged.

Sheikh took his hand away. He spoke into a
radio nestled into his jacket. Some kind of code
word. Harry waited.

'Police don't come around here, you know.'

A door opened and there was a brief but noisy
burst of Arabic music. A smart-looking Middle-
Eastern man, maybe early thirties, in a striking
black suit, stood at the entrance. Sheikh briefed
him.

'May I see some ID,' said the man to Harry.

Harry showed it.

'What can I help you with, Detective?'

'Your name to start with.'

'Yousef.'

'Mind if I come inside, Yousef?'

'May I ask why?'

'No.'

'Then my answer must also be no.' He spoke
softly and politely.

Harry nodded. 'Thing is, if I rock up here
with a warrant, a van full of armed police and a
reporter or two, this really small thing I'm trying to do is going to become a big thing.'

'This is a private members' club. Without a warrant, I'm afraid I cannot let you in,' said Yousef.

Harry took out his police-issue radio. It was switched off but they didn't know that. He started to speak into it, asking for a squad car and an armed patrol unit.

Yousef acted quickly.

'OK, OK,' he said, putting his hands together as if in prayer. 'Please, let us start over.'

Harry spoke into his radio and cancelled the car and patrol unit, thankful these guys had no idea he was bluffing.

'What is it you want, Detective?' said Yousef, beckoning for Harry to follow him.

'Just a look around.'

Harry followed Yousef into the club. Red velvet couches, oak-panelled walls and dim lighting. Harry imagined the type of chat that went on here. Truthfully, it was inviting. If it had been any other place, Harry would have enjoyed a drink here.

'So, what are you looking for?' asked Yousef.

'I'm looking for a guy called Zak Choudary. Do you know him?'

Yousef didn't reply, as if thinking how best to answer.

'It's a private members' club, Yousef. I imagine

51

that means form-filling. Everyone knows everyone. It's not a difficult question. Either you know him or you don't.'

Yousef nodded. 'I know the name.'

'Is he here?'

Again, Yousef didn't move and said nothing.

'Mind if I have a look around?' said Harry.

'I do mind, Mr Virdee. But feel free to explore. I would offer you a drink, but I'm afraid only members can have drinks.'

Harry smiled and walked away.

Each table had a shisha pipe and a built-in iPad. Harry glanced at one. A menu, for ordering. That was pretty plush for a place in Bradford.

This place stank of black money – drug money.

Harry sat down on a red Chesterfield couch. The club had a few guests, their eyes all on Harry as if there were a sign above his head, *Police*. Nobody looked concerned.

A young man Harry instantly recognized from his police file as Zak Choudary emerged from the shadows and strode across to him.

'Yo, heard you is looking for me,' he said, shrugging his shoulders. The arrogance was startling.

Harry stayed seated, looking him over. There was nothing to him. He was skin and bones, a little under six foot.

Zak nodded to a room towards the back.

'Privacy? Or you want to talk here?'

Harry stood up. 'Privacy seems right.'

'Let's do this, amigo.'

Zak walked away and Harry followed.

They entered a small room with two couches on either side. Zak closed the door.

'Don't get many pigs in here.'

Harry turned to face him. 'How would you know? You haven't been out that long.'

'You know the score. Pigs don't come here.'

Harry glanced around the room, looking for cameras, but found none. A large one-way window gave a view outside where Harry saw the bouncer, Sheikh, now walking in. He had a bad feeling about this.

Zak stepped aside and Sheikh entered, closing the door.

Nobody said anything. Harry got the message.

'Really?' he said, looking at Zak, who smirked and sat down, spreading his arms across the back of the couch like a mafia boss.

'Policing is changing in this country, man. Shit, when I was growing up, coppers used to give you a smack round the head. We saw you lot and we ran. There was a system in place – an order, everyone understood it.'

He looked up at Harry, who was still standing up.

'Now, the dealers, we control the streets.'

Zak just confessed to being a dealer. He was either stupid or he had a plan.

'You wearing a wire, Detective? Legally, you need to tell me if you are.'

Harry shook his head, getting annoyed.

Zak nodded at Sheikh, who stepped towards Harry.

'You best back away, Big Man,' said Harry.

'You want to talk openly or you want to piss off?'

Harry allowed Sheikh to frisk him.

'Clean,' Sheikh said to Zak.

Zak stood up. His manner changed. 'How much do you want?'

Harry said nothing.

'Everyone's got a price. We're always looking for good people.'

'You got the wrong man.'

Zak closed the gap between them, as if to threaten Harry.

'You step to me, in this place, and you're not here for a number? What? You think you're leaving in one piece? If you are, it's because I put this in your pocket.'

Zak removed a large wedge of cash from his pocket. Harry glanced at it.

'You don't want it? Well then, maybe life's going

to start getting difficult for you.' Zak pointed out-side. 'People talk. And nobody comes into my house, steps to me and doesn't walk out on the take. There's a drug war coming, everyone knows it. Whose side do you want to be on?'

His tone, his manner, everything about him was pissing Harry off.

'I'm here about two murders. We can either do this here or down the nick.'

Zak smiled, then started to laugh. He turned and walked away, pacing around the small room, shaking his head. He came back to Harry.

'I dropped a couple of bodies. Sure. There's a new kid in town and everyone is going to know about it. Thing is, without proof – you can't do shit, can you, Detective?'

'You've got a big mouth, haven't you?'

'Your word against mine.' Zak turned to Sheikh. 'Yo, you hear this pig saying he was going to stitch me up? Say I did two murders?'

'That's what I heard.'

Zak smiled. 'I reckon there's a few more people out there who heard it too. You get me, Detective?'

Zak stepped a little closer, the smell of mari-juana on his clothes.

'I run these streets as I want. You get back to handing out parking tickets and leave this shit alone. Otherwise, bad things sometimes happen to good people.'

Sheikh came closer, perhaps sensing that Harry was becoming anxious.

'Either take the cash and we become friends. Or. Get. The. Fuck. Out.'

Harry closed the gap a little more, both of them now eye-to-eye.

'Little boys like you come and go, Zak. In the end, you will see a cell. Then some other prick will step into your shoes and we will start over again.'

Zak smiled. 'Get some evidence first, rookie.' He backed away and said to Sheikh, 'Toss him the fuck outside.'

Harry was marched outside with his arm twisted behind his back.

Everyone inside the club witnessed it. A message that, in this city, police were nothing.

Outside, Sheikh took Harry round the back to a dark alleyway full of bins and rubbish and threw him on to the dirty cobbles.

Harry got up. Sheikh was goading him into a fight.

On any other day, Harry might have taken him on. Now, it was getting late. He thought of Saima, at home, getting ready for the wedding reception they needed to attend. Harry walked away.

Chapter Ten

Harry was alone in his living room, standing in darkness by the window. He found it calming to watch the world go by. He often wondered what people might be hiding, what traumas were hidden inside *their* souls. Perhaps he had been working in Bradford too long. Or perhaps it was because of what his marriage to Saima had cost him. Either way, this was what he did to wind down. He tried to remove the day's events from his mind. Tonight, for a short while at least, he would forget about Zak Choudary. Never before had Harry heard a dealer so brazenly confess to his crimes. He thought he was too powerful to fail. One thing was certain – more bodies were likely to follow.

Harry closed his eyes. He had to stop thinking about this shit. Tonight was going to be tough. His focus needed to be on the wedding. He and Saima couldn't hide from these occasions for ever.

Asian weddings were lavish occasions, full of pomp and ceremony. Harry had no personal experience of it. He had married Saima at Bradford register office with only two witnesses.

They should have had their families there. But Harry had been threatened with death, and Saima's father had dragged her by the hair and thrown her into the street. Harry and Saima Virdee had lost everything in order to be together.

Religious bullshit, as far as Harry was concerned. He had been raised here, in the UK, and age-old hatred stemming from the 1947 partition of India did not matter to him like it did to the older generation.

But some part of Harry had died – the bond with his family.

Tonight, after almost three years, he was going to come face-to-face with not only his parents but also the Sikh community they belonged to. A wedding to celebrate his friend's arranged marriage, it would also remind Harry what he had denied his own parents.

Saima's voice broke into his thoughts.

'Are you going to stand there all night or give me a hand with this?'

He turned and couldn't help but smile at the sight of his heavily pregnant wife, her body squeezed into a glistening orange Asian suit. The zip was stuck halfway up her back and one of her breasts was bulging out from the side.

'You look . . . hot,' said Harry, folding his arms across his chest.

Keeping her back towards him, Saima turned her head and frowned. 'Does it look like I am having fun?'

'I'm pretty certain a nice maternity outfit would have done.'

'First impressions matter. Remember? Well, are you going to help me?'

Harry went up to her and stared at the zip. He couldn't see how it would close.

'Saima, this isn't going to—'

'I'm going to breathe in and then you try it.'

'Breathe in? You're nine months' pregnant. That's not going to work.'

'Wait,' she said, standing up, readying herself.

Harry was about to object when she took an enormous breath. It made no difference to the zip.

'Saima, it's not working.'

She murmured for him to try harder, still holding her breath.

Harry grabbed the zip but the damn thing wouldn't budge.

Saima breathed out heavily. 'I'm not made of glass, Harry, get on with it! Give it another pull.'

Harry did so, and this time the end came off in his hand and the zipper slowly started to unfasten.

'Harry! What did you do?'

He came round to face her as the outfit slid off

59

her shoulders. Harry whistled. 'On any other day, I would say this was a striptease.'

She frowned at him.

Harry tried to hide his smile. 'You should see yourself – belly sticking out, granny knickers pulled high and those compression stockings . . .' Harry whistled. 'I've never wanted you more.'

'Piss off. What are we going to do now?'

'Put another outfit on?'

'It's the first time I'm going to see your parents. People from your community. I can't look like a clown.'

'The Asian fashion stores will still be open. Crisis shopping trip?'

Saima stepped past him. 'Get your wallet, Virdee. You're paying.'

Chapter Eleven

Harry was parked in the Bradford Hotel car park looking at a row of Bentleys, all done up with red ribbon. One had a sign on it. *Just Married.*

Saima put her hand on his. 'We don't have to do this if you really don't want to.'

Harry thought of what else he might be doing – he would be at the office with Palmer working the Zak Choudary case. He wondered if any progress had been made.

'Hey,' said Saima.

Harry faced her, unable to find a smile. She looked wonderful in a new red Asian suit with matching bangles and necklace. Thoughts of work disappeared.

Being here was one thing. Entering the Bradford Hotel with a heavily pregnant Saima was quite something else.

What would people think of him?

He hated that he was even thinking it. He forced a smile. 'Like you said, can't hide for ever.'

'You are here to celebrate your friend's wedding.

You two have been close since you were teenagers. That is what this is about. Nothing else.'

Harry stared again at the row of expensive cars. 'I'm worried we might come face-to-face with Mum and Dad.'

'If it happens, we will be very British and greet them politely.'

Harry thought of his mother's slippers in his hallway. If he saw her tonight, would she step away if he went to touch her feet?

Saima put her hand on his face and turned it towards her. 'Like I said, if it's too difficult, we don't have to go inside. We can return this outfit, bank the money and go for a spicy curry at Mughal's.' She rubbed her tummy. 'Might make this one get a move on.'

Harry switched off the engine. 'There's free food here.'

Harry held Saima's hand tightly as they stepped into the banqueting suite of the Bradford Hotel. The room was vibrating, dozens of people dancing to a Bhangra beat. Strobe lighting bounced from the DJ station and the dance floor was filled with colourful saris.

He scanned the other names on his table.

All white.

Harry relaxed.

He saw his parents' names were on a table near the front.

They moved through the crowd, slowly, Harry feeling Saima's hand tighten around his. This felt alien, to be out in public in a place where his entire community was present. His father had been the president of the Sikh Society in Bradford, stepping down in shame once news had broken of what Harry had done.

They sat down at their table and nodded to the eight other people already there. Harry checked the time. The dancing would stop in around fifteen minutes and give way to dinner.

He was still holding Saima's hand when she leaned in and said, 'We good?', raising her voice over the deafening music.

Harry suddenly felt a strong hand on his shoulder. He turned to see his friend, Jag, standing there with his new wife, beaming at him, clearly a little drunk.

Harry stood up, and Saima followed.

'What time do you call this, Virdee?' said Jag, hugging him and slapping him on the back.

'Asian timing, friend.'

Jag pulled away and introduced his wife, Balvinder, who smiled and shook Harry's hand.

'This is the guy I was telling you about. My boy, Harry.'

'Congratulations,' said Harry, noticing that she, too, looked a little drunk.

'I've heard a lot about you,' said Balvinder, then turned to Saima. 'And you must be Mrs Virdee. I've heard a lot about you too.'

'And you also,' replied Saima, putting out her hand, which Jag shook before his wife did the same.

'Dance?' shouted Jag, pointing to the dance floor.

'Not if my life depended on it,' said Harry.

'Mrs Virdee?' said Jag to Saima.

She put her hands on her tummy. 'Another time?'

Jag waved his hand at them both. 'Before this night is out, I'm hitting that dance floor with you both – no excuses!'

He patted Harry on the shoulder and moved back towards the head table as the DJ announced that food was about to be served. The music died out, the crowd on the dance floor moved away. Softer music now streamed through the speakers. Waiters came into the room, carrying sizzling trays of Asian food.

The lights came up a little, making Harry nervous. No more hiding in the shadows. He dropped his gaze, focused on the table.

'You don't need to look anywhere else, Harry

Virdee. You can just look at me and' – she pointed to her stomach – 'Rehanna.'

Harry relaxed, shook his head and said, 'Veto.'

Harry was at the bar, dinner well under way. Saima had bonded with the lady sitting next to her, who was also a nurse, but at Leeds not Bradford. He had left them both discussing their jobs.

The waiter put Harry's shot of Jack Daniels in front of him and refused payment. It was a free bar, as usual at a lavish Asian wedding.

'It must be a really bad night if Harry Virdee is standing alone at the bar with, let me guess, bourbon on ice,' said a voice from behind him. Harry sighed. He knew that voice.

The woman ordered a neat whisky for herself. Harry gulped his drink and put the empty glass on the bar.

'And give him the same again,' she said.

'No thanks,' said Harry, raising his hand at the barman. He still hadn't turned to face the woman.

'So you will fuck me, Harry Virdee, but you won't let me buy you a drink?'

'It's a free bar, Deepi,' he said.

'Look at me.'

Harry didn't. Out of the corner of his eye, he caught a glimpse of her body. She was wearing an elegant bright yellow Asian suit, gleaming with diamantes. He could smell her perfume, the familiar scent of Chanel.

Deepi lowered her voice and added some bite. 'Look. At. Me.'

This was the last thing Harry needed. He turned his head ever so slightly.

She looked the same. The eye-catching girl, desired by many Sikh households as the perfect daughter-in-law. But her destiny had always been tied to Harry's. For years their families had spoken of them getting married – a friendship that would blossom into family. It was not quite the arranged marriage that Harry dreaded. They had even dated.

But Harry had broken with tradition.

'You look well,' said Harry, unable to think of anything else.

She gave him a long and thoughtful look. When it was clear she wasn't going to say anything, Harry tried to move away. But she grabbed his arm.

'No you fucking don't.'

'Don't make a scene, Deepi. Not here.'

'First time I see you in years and you think you can just walk away? Again?'

'It was so long ago, can't we just . . .'

Deepi drank her whisky in one gulp. He had dated her for over a year and had never known her to drink neat whisky.

'Is *she* here?' said Deepi, slamming the empty glass on the bar.

Harry didn't reply. He glanced round and saw her father, Pardeep, in the distance, watching.

He tried to move away and again she stopped him, this time digging her nails harder into his arm.

'What do you want?' said Harry.

'I want to meet her.'

'No.'

'Why not?'

'Because I said so.' Harry leaned closer to her, the perfume again assaulting his senses. The image of her naked body rolling around a bed with him flashed across his mind. 'Let go of me.'

'I won't. Not until I meet her.'

'Why, Deepi? What good could it possibly do?'

'I want to know exactly what that bitch has that I don't have. I want to see the woman who ruined my life.'

Harry lost his patience, grabbed her hand and forcefully removed it from his arm. He moved closer, so their lips were almost touching, and whispered, 'You really want to know what Saima has that you don't?'

She nodded, defiant.

'Everything,' he said.

Chapter Twelve

Zak Choudary once again found himself staring on to the disorder that was Great Horton Road from the first floor of the kebab takeaway. The boss had summoned him almost immediately.

'The thing I'm asking myself, Zak, is do you know what the fuck you are doing?'

'I do.'

'Really? Big man Sheikh tells me you told a detective that you dropped a couple of bodies. Are you stupid?'

Zak smiled. 'No, I am not.'

'Explain.'

Zak didn't have to force the self-belief in his voice. He told him that the detective could not be turned with a bribe. And Zak hadn't wanted to play the usual game of being accused of a crime and denying it. No, he had told the detective what he needed to hear. That in this city Zak Choudary controlled the streets and there wasn't a fucking thing the police could do about it. He needed the detective to leave knowing Zak was no ordinary criminal.

'There was another reason,' said Zak.

'Go on.'

'Big man Sheikh heard me say it. Then everyone saw him march that pig out of the club and toss him outside. They will all be talking about it now. How I faced the cops and I am still standing. I will still be standing because, unlike the police, these streets aren't a job to me. They are everything. I don't leave evidence and I don't have witnesses. Word will soon get across to those Bradford-East bastards about what happened, and everyone will know my name. My reputation. You wanted war. You will have it.'

Zak finished his speech and waited.

He heard a muted laugh from behind. 'I knew when I recruited you that it would be all or nothing. You're pushing hard.'

'Only way to be.' Zak pointed to the street below. 'Everyone needs to know my name. They need to whisper it, like saying it loudly might get them hurt.'

Zak turned round and moved closer to his boss. He could clearly see his boss's face. 'Brother, you hooked me up. Gave me a chance. There is only one thing I want. To repay you so that, one day, you will trust me enough to be sitting where you are, so I can find my own Zak Choudarys.'

His boss smiled, an almost cruel expression. 'And if this detective is more than you expected?'

'The pigs on our payroll already told me where he's at. Oak Lane. Got a pregnant wife and lots to lose. He won't push too hard.'

'And if he does?'

Zak pointed behind him towards Great Horton Road. 'Then I will let him know that was a mistake.'

Chapter Thirteen

Harry was ready to go home but Saima refused. After speeches and another round of Bhangra, they were now preparing for the wedding to reach its finale.

Harry had not wanted to stay for this, the most emotional part. The *bidaai* involved a lot of crying, as the bride prepared to leave her family home to enter her husband's.

The guests lined each side of the foyer, many standing outside, where the Bentley was waiting to whisk the bride and groom away to start their new life. A traditional song started to play, the words piercing Harry's ears.

'Let me take my father's blessings with me as I leave this house . . .'

The bride appeared, walking behind her husband, head bowed. Each step drew a sob from the bride and her family. The groom also kept his head down. With every step, the bride threw a handful of rice behind her, to thank her parents for feeding and looking after her.

Women in the foyer were crying, no doubt remembering when they did this. Saima cried too. Although she had never taken such a walk, Harry knew she was thinking of her family.

Harry held her hand tightly.

'We don't have to stay for this,' he whispered.

She shook her head and stood absolutely still, tears creeping down her face.

Harry didn't like it one bit. She was about to give birth. This was not the right time to get worked up about a past they could not change.

'Let me watch,' she whispered.

As the bride passed them, Harry saw the one person he had hoped to avoid. His mother, Joyti, on the other side of the room.

Their eyes met. Joyti was looking straight at Harry, crying.

He swallowed hard, unable to look away. He gripped Saima's hand harder.

The bride reached the hotel exit and stepped outside. The foyer emptied with her and the sad music stopped playing.

Harry and Saima remained where they were, as did Joyti Virdee. The three of them stood there awkwardly.

'My mum,' whispered Harry to Saima.

He didn't know what to do.

He looked around for his father but he was nowhere to be seen.

Joyti walked towards them. Saima was still crying.

'*Puthar*,' said Joyti, stopping right in front of Harry.

Son.

A voice – a word – he craved. It had been three years since he had heard it.

Harry thought of the slippers resting on the table inside his house.

There was a moment of stillness.

Then Harry stooped and touched his mother's feet.

Saima looked at him, amazed. It wasn't an Islamic tradition and she was not familiar with it. Yet she too tried to bend down, her pregnant belly getting in the way.

Joyti moved to stop her.

'Don't be silly. You don't need to do that,' said Joyti.

'But I do,' said Saima. 'I must.'

Joyti stroked Saima's hair – an act of blessing. 'Bless you, my child,' she said in Punjabi.

Harry saw Saima's lip quivering as she wiped her face.

Joyti placed her hands on Saima's tummy. 'Stop your crying. It is no good for this baby. I had heard my Hardeep was about to become a father,' she said softly.

73

Saima put her hands on top of Joyti's. 'Please don't be mad with us,' she said.

Joyti smiled, shook her head and said nothing. She kept her hands on Saima a little longer, then turned to Harry and put one hand on each side of his face. 'When I woke up this morning, my heart was broken. It is still broken. It will stay broken for a long time. But now I have seen you, tonight, I will not wonder as much how you are.'

Harry hugged her.

Joyti pulled away. 'I have to go, before your father realizes where I am.'

Harry didn't object. There was no point. This was how it was.

Joyti was hiding something in her hands and now showed it to Harry. A small packet of sugar from the hotel. She tore it open and waited.

Harry shook his head. 'Really?'

Joyti wiped her face. She wouldn't last much longer without breaking down.

Harry smiled and stepped towards her, crouching a little. Joyti poured some sugar into her hand. She had done this ever since he could remember – before exams, a big rugby match, a difficult case he was handling.

She sprinkled the sugar into his mouth.

'Be blessed,' she said. She turned to Saima, who followed Harry's lead and allowed Joyti to do it for her.

Then, as happened the last time Harry saw her, his mother turned and walked away.

Chapter Fourteen

Harry was once again standing by his window in the living room. He wanted a drink – a big one – but with Saima overdue, he couldn't risk not being able to drive.

His chest ached, as if his lungs were being squeezed. His breathing was heavy and hard.

This was why he didn't go to Asian functions. There was always a sense of betrayal because of what he had done. They had all been raised going to grand weddings like the one he had been to. The promise was that one day his family would celebrate such an occasion.

He folded his arms across his chest, rested his head on the window frame and closed his eyes.

On a night like this, he could not help but think of the past.

Would his father really have killed him?

'Why are you thinking of those times?' came Saima's voice from behind him.

Harry opened his eyes. 'I'm just watching the world go by.'

'Liar.'

She arrived by his side, wearing a loose night-gown. The moonlight caught the side of her face as she looked at Harry.

He smiled at her, pained.

Her face was serious. Beautiful.

She unfolded his arms and stepped into an embrace. Harry wrapped his arms around her and they just stood there.

Saima slipped her hands under Harry's shirt and ran them over his skin.

'It's OK to feel this way,' she whispered.

He said nothing.

'You're only human. Not a machine.'

'I did this. It's on me.'

'No. We did this. Nobody forced you to marry me.'

'You did. That bloody nurse's uniform.'

'Such a bloke,' she said, moving her hand round to his chest and resting it over his heart.

'Still beating?' he said.

'Strong.'

Harry kissed the top of her head. 'How was it tonight? Seeing Mum for the first time.'

'She was . . . I don't know . . . kind.'

'Don't sound so surprised. She isn't my father.'

Saima pulled away from him. 'Do you think he saw us?'

Harry shrugged. 'I don't know.'

77

'Do you think . . . we should move? Once the baby arrives? Leave all these memories behind. Start a new life.'

Harry had thought about it. In fact, there wasn't a day when he didn't. 'Is that what you want, Saima?'

'I don't want you always standing here like this. Alone. Hurting.'

'Always? When was the last time?'

She raised her eyebrows.

'Bradford . . . needs me.' His thoughts momentarily went to Zak Choudary and the brazen way he had spoken to him.

'Does it? Maybe you need Bradford.'

Harry smiled. 'What are you now? A psychiatrist?'

She sat on the window ledge. 'Truth?'

'Always.'

'Maybe you love this city because it's the only thing more damaged than you are.'

Harry looked away.

Eventually he said, 'It's just . . . home, Saima.'

'I saw it today, Harry. The hurt. In you. In your mother. I did that. I caused that.'

He turned to face her. 'Don't say that. Ever.'

His tone was sharper than he intended. He put his hands on her stomach. 'Let's end this night on a positive. I have a winner.'

She rolled her eyes. 'Go on.'

'Ava.'

'Ava Virdee?'

'Exactly.'

Saima tipped her head to one side. 'Veto. It's too white.'

Chapter Fifteen

Harry stepped out of the house at 5 a.m.

He ran harder than usual, punishing himself. A sleepless night thinking about his mother had now given way to thoughts about work.

Zak Choudary and trying to close this damn case. Simpson's words were clear in Harry's mind.

You bring this home quickly and quietly, Harry, and I will owe you.

He had seldom heard such pain in his boss's voice. The East–West drug war had the potential to explode and destroy Bradford.

He arrived back at the house to find Saima still asleep. Would today be the day their baby girl arrived? They really needed to find a name.

Harry showered, got changed and was in the kitchen making a coffee, thinking about work. It was going to be tough to nail Zak and stay on the right side of the law. Not that that bothered him. In Bradford, you had to bend the rules to get things done.

His phone rang.

Unknown number.

Harry answered, as he added a new name to the chart in the kitchen.

Olivia.

'Harry Virdee esquire,' said a voice Harry knew all too well. His heart sank. Harry closed his eyes and shook his head. The case with Zak Choudary was about to get really, really messy.

'Christ, it's as bad as that?' said Harry.

'It could be. Come and see me after nine.'

Harry arrived at Viper Prestige Cars at the bottom end of Sticker Lane at two minutes to nine. It only traded elite vehicles – Ferraris, Porsches and the like. Harry parked in a customer bay, shaking his head. He would love one of these cars, but he would only be able to afford one if he joined the bad guys.

The shop's interior was a sleek, cool design. White marble tiles covered the floor and a large canopy hung from the ceiling, giving off a warm orange glow. Massive plasma TV screens on the walls showed some of the luxury cars being driven round a race track.

Harry checked in at the desk. Before he could finish, he heard a booming voice above his head.

Owais Patel was, at one time, the most notorious drug-dealer in Bradford. He had never been convicted of any crimes – always too smart to get caught. Although he hid behind this garage, every detective in the city knew that he was still the boss of the Bradford-East drug gang. Owais had caused a dozen deaths, directly or indirectly, stretching back almost a decade. Always one step ahead and with enough money to ensure nobody ever spoke against him, he was as clean as they got. A lot of his men had been jailed recently, which must have hurt his reach. Harry hadn't heard from him since.

Harry took the stairs to his office.

The men didn't shake hands and, as Harry sat down, he heard a magnetic lock behind him. The door was bolted.

'Like that, is it?' he asked.

Owais was a huge man. Six foot five and almost three hundred pounds with tattoos creeping up both arms. He was wearing a tight T-shirt, biceps bulging.

'I'm locking the door because I don't want to be disturbed when I've got DI Harry Virdee in the house. Big man like you deserves my full attention. Now, tea? Coffee?'

'Receptionist already asked. I'm good.'

'You look well. Still hitting the rugby pitches on Saturday mornings?'

Harry shrugged. 'Less these days. Mostly running around after low-lifes.'

Owais laughed. 'No doubt there. Drugs still run this city.' He said it as if it upset him, like he knew nothing about it. Harry reckoned he would have pissed over any lie detector.

'What can I do for you, Owais?' said Harry. He didn't want to be here any longer than he needed to be.

'I heard on the grapevine a couple of Bradford-East boys died on the streets lately,' said Owais, shaking his head. 'We are all trying to clean this city up, best way we can, and these low-lifes start dropping bodies. Anything I can help with?'

Harry smiled.

He was used to these loaded conversations.

'Help?' he said, playing along.

'You know how I am. I try to help the young-sters stay clean. Why do you think I fund the community outreach programme at Bradford College? So, is some young lad wanting to make a name for himself? Want me to ask around? Stop this before Bradford-East replies? That shit might get out of hand.'

And there it was. The threat.

Owais's face remained blank.

Harry sucked his teeth. 'I think we've been playing this game long enough, Owais. You can just get to the point.'

'OK,' said Owais, getting up from his seat and

coming around to Harry. He sat on the desk and dropped his voice.

'I'm hearing about some Bradford-West new-bie. I don't think we've had a drug war in a while. Not one that littered the streets with bodies any-way. You got – what? – two now? Killed in the same way, I'm hearing. Bad times,' said Owais, shaking his head. 'If Bradford-East replies in kind, we might have the start of a shit-storm. Nobody wants that.'

Owais stared at Harry and Harry stared back. The silence stretched to almost a minute.

'The question I have for you, Harry, is this. How close are you to bringing this home?'

Harry finally looked away. He said nothing.

Owais shrugged. 'I'm trying to help here. Nobody wants this to get any worse, but if another guy hits the pavement, Bradford-East might fight back. So, seeing as I do a lot of *community work* with youth, I'm asking you, are you on top of this? Or do I need to ask some questions and try to help you out?'

Harry got to his feet. He had got the message. 'I'm on it.'

Harry walked away. He reached the door and stopped.

'How long before Bradford-East loses patience?' he said.

'You're asking the wrong man, Harry. But knowing how this city works, I will take a punt. I would say you've got another twenty-four hours.' Owais released the magnetic lock.

Harry was in the parking lot when he checked his phone. Several missed calls from Saima and a text.

Something not right with baby. I need you.

Chapter Sixteen

Harry arrived home to find an ambulance outside.

He rushed in. Saima was sitting at their dining table, paramedics either side.

She looked pale and frightened. She hadn't answered any of his calls from the car.

'What's wrong? What happened?' he asked urgently.

One of the paramedics raised a hand. 'Nothing, nothing, just some aches and pregnancy-related pains.'

'Saima?' said Harry, crouching beside her.

He could tell she was annoyed that he hadn't answered his phone.

'I was in a meeting, Saima,' he said. 'Please, what is it?'

'I had some pains and . . . I haven't felt the baby move since last night.'

Last night. He should have insisted they left that damn wedding early.

Harry looked at one of the paramedics, who was packing some equipment away.

'We are going to take her in. A few routine checks.'

'OK,' said Harry, standing up and helping Saima to her feet.

'I'm really sorry,' he said. 'I ... I ... had my phone on silent.'

'It's fine,' she replied, smiling. 'Let's just get into hospital.'

Saima worked as a nurse in A&E at Bradford Royal Infirmary, so she knew the staff and got the five-star treatment. She was checked into the neo-natal unit almost immediately.

The baby's heart was beating strongly. Even so, they were going to keep Saima under observation for a few hours, to make sure all was well – and, he thought, to comfort her.

Harry phoned into work and told Palmer he was going to be busy for the next few hours. He hoped to get in a little later. They were working with skeleton staff as it was.

For now, Harry Virdee was going to do nothing except be with his wife.

But he couldn't shake the thought of what Owais had threatened.

Chapter Seventeen

Harry ordered Saima a spicy curry on the way home. The baby was healthy, but the doctors had threatened an induced labour in the next couple of days. Saima didn't want that.

Harry had missed a full day on the Zak Choudary case. Palmer had kept him updated, but he needed to be out there, doing something. Saima sensed his concern.

'Why don't you go into work tonight?' she suggested.

Harry didn't want to leave her, not after today. But his mind was made up for him when he found an envelope in his hallway.

No postage stamp.

Hand delivered.

Harry opened it and found a large wedge of cash and a hand-written note.

You look like you might need this. Pregnant wife, shitty cop's salary. We could be good friends. Look after this city. Enjoy this. Buy the kid some toys. Plenty more where it came from.

There was no signature but Harry knew damn well who it was from.

The message was clear.

Zak knew where he lived. He knew about his life.

This was a threat.

This was personal.

Harry left the house, promising to keep his phone on all night. As he walked to his car, the phone began to ring.

Saima checking on him, he thought.

But it wasn't his wife.

'You're kidding me?' he said, but there was no conviction in his voice.

Harry closed his eyes and rested his body against his car. 'Which hospital?'

Harry arrived on the Surgical Assessment Unit of Bradford Royal Infirmary fifteen minutes later.

Natalie Zurek was asleep in her bed, her face badly bruised and swollen. According to the staff, she had three broken ribs.

Harry grabbed a chair and brought it to the side of the bed. This close, he could see the damage in detail. Zak Choudary.

Harry put his head in his hands. He should have insisted on the panic alarms.

'Looks worse than it is,' mumbled Natalie.

Harry looked up. One of her eyes was closed, swollen.

Harry thought about the promise he had made to get her to speak about Zak – to protect her. He felt numb.

'Natalie, I'm sorry. I don't know what else to say.'

'You didn't do this.'

'No. But I know who did.'

'I didn't see the guy.' The words were an effort for her. 'I told them.'

Harry had been briefed on his way over. Natalie had apparently been unloading supermarket shopping from her car when she had been attacked by a faceless stranger. But there were no packed shopping bags at her home.

Harry put his hand on the bed and held hers gently.

'This isn't right, Natalie.'

'I know,' she whispered.

Harry sighed deeply. 'I get it. I've been here many times with other people. Just do me one small thing?'

She nodded.

'If it was who we spoke about last time we met, squeeze my hand and I'll make sure you never have to see him again.'

Natalie turned her face away from Harry.

Then she squeezed his hand.

90

Chapter Eighteen

Harry was in a rage as he pulled his car to the side of the road near Arabian Delightz.

Natalie in hospital was bad enough, but the fact Zak or one of his mates had dared to approach Harry's house? That was a step too far.

Focus, Harry. Work it through, carefully. Put what you need into play.

He got out, walked along Thornton Road and, before he knew it, he had reached the side-street where the Crabtree Mill was.

Where he had met Shelley the day before.

Harry glanced back towards the club, then the mill, then his car.

He took out his phone and called Shelley.

'It's late,' she said.

'I know. Are you at the Crabtree building?'

'I'm out, Harry. Working.'

'Where?'

'Why are you asking?'

'I want to buy an hour of your time.'

She didn't reply and Harry saw his error. 'Not for that.'

'Time is money. Up to you how you spend it.'

'I will pick you up.'

Shelley got into Harry's car. Like Thornton Road, Lumb Lane had, in times gone by, been a notorious red-light spot.

'Didn't think this area worked this way any more,' said Harry.

'It doesn't. Not like it used to. But we got regulars that can't be bothered going into Leeds.'

Prostitution had been given a protected area in Leeds where girls could work and punters could roam without either side being arrested. It had almost wiped out the trade in Bradford.

Harry parked on a side-street.

Shelley cocked her head to one side.

'I'm here for Zak,' said Harry.

'Meaning?'

'There's a way I can get to him.'

'Do it then.'

'I need your help.'

'How so?' Shelley looked nervous. She started playing with her hands.

'I need you to get Emily to help me.'

Shelley shook her head. 'No way. You know how scared she is of Zak?'

'I know.'

Harry told her what had happened to Natalie. 'I'm afraid that's what Emily has coming, too.' Shelley's eyes filled with tears. One hand clawed at the other. Harry put his hand over hers. 'Trust me, Shelley. I can get to him, but it isn't strictly above board.'

'What kind of police officer are you?' she asked.

'One who gets shit done. One who wants Zak Choudary put away.'

He immediately wished he hadn't said that last part.

'Why?' she asked.

Harry paused. Shelley wouldn't care that Zak knew where he lived. She wouldn't care about his wife or his unborn child. He needed to focus on Shelley's family here, not his own.

'He's dangerous. I'm afraid that at some point Emily is going to be in the firing line, just like Natalie. You do see that, right? She's afraid of him and rightly so. He goes away, her life gets back to normal.'

Shelley was chewing her lip.

She wanted this. Harry could see it. Emily was her little sister. She would do anything to keep her safe.

'Come on, Shelley. I only need one shot. And after this, you would officially be my informant and that means nobody is fucking around with you or with Emily. Deal?'

Shelley looked out of the window, across the street. 'OK,' she replied. 'I will do it.'

Chapter Nineteen

An hour later.

Harry was standing in a doorway off Lumb Lane, about a hundred yards away from Shelley, who was loitering by the side of the street.

Waiting.

The street lights were out. Harry was practically invisible to anyone walking or driving by. He watched as a shitty old Nissan pulled up by the kerb.

Zak Choudary. Shelley spoke to the driver then got inside.

Harry waited, almost holding his breath.

Less than five minutes later, Shelley was back on the pavement huddled against the rain.

Harry waited until she had walked away in the other direction before heading back to his car.

He checked his phone as he started the car.

It was Shelley.

He bought it.

'Of course he did,' whispered Harry to himself.

Chapter Twenty

Zak Choudary was feeling pretty damn good. The bag of heroin he had just got would do that. Easy money.

He was in Emily's apartment at the top of the new Lister Mills complex, standing on the balcony. From here, he had one of the finest views across the city, his city. In under eight weeks, Zak had taken out two of the Bradford-East gang. The bosses were happy. Even that rookie detective would come round. Zak had seen it in his eyes. It was only a matter of time.

And he had more planned. Those Bradford-East bastards wouldn't know what had hit them.

And now this. Emily's pathetic sister, Shelley, had seen a fight between two Bradford-East dealers. One of them had thrown something on to the embankment off Thornton Road.

Half a kilo of heroin.

Shelley had called Emily, who had seen an opportunity. She wanted a 50/50 split. But there was no way he was going to keep that promise.

Zak finished smoking his cigarette and went into the bathroom. He opened a cabinet, removed a small bottle of blue pills and popped a Viagra. He had left Emily in the bedroom and told her to be ready for him. Zak turned on the shower feeling ecstatic.

Zak Choudary left the shower only when the water had started to run cold. Goddamn it, he had missed this kind of luxury.

He wrapped a towel around his waist. Right now, he felt as good as he had done since he had come out of prison. Viagra kicking in, a woman waiting, money on the way.

He opened the bathroom door and went into the living room, but stopped dead when he found two uniformed officers standing there, next to Emily.

The bag of heroin was still on the coffee table.

Zak looked at Emily.

Standing there, naked except for a towel, slowly realizing he wasn't about to enjoy the benefits of the blue pill, Zak Choudary sat down on the leather couch, folded his arms across his chest and said, 'Lawyer.'

Chapter Twenty-one

It was past midnight when Zak was brought into the station. Harry had him taken into an interview room. The handcuffs stayed on.

He sat down opposite Zak.

'You haven't got shit on me.' He smiled up at Harry.

Harry kept a straight face. 'Thing with you lot is . . . the drugs, the money, the women. In the end, you all end up in here.'

'You set this up, pig?'

Harry shrugged. 'No idea what you mean by that.'

'Fuck me. When I get out of here, you and I are going to spend some time together. You know?' Zak smiled but it didn't reach his eyes.

'I don't think so, Son. You are going nowhere except a cell.' Harry leaned back, crossing his arms over his chest.

'I ain't your son.'

'Two dead bodies, half a kilo of heroin and you're still on probation. That's some re-entry to the world.'

'Dead bodies? You better be able to prove that shit.'

'I can't.'

Zak smiled.

Harry leaned forward. 'But the heroin, that's all on you.'

Zak rocked back on his chair. 'That shit was there when I got there. Whore set me up.'

Harry shook his head. 'That will never wash. You've got prior convictions. She's clean. Anyway, there's CCTV all over that complex, dozens of cameras, inside and out. And if that's not enough, I just spoke to Emily and she is one sharp operator. You see, she has this tiny portable camera in her apartment. Back in the days when she wasn't exclusive to you, she used it to video clients coming and going in case anyone got cute with her. Now, I've had a look at that footage and all I can see is you walking in with the heroin, laughing your ass off.'

Zak's expression changed.

Harry smiled.

'She's prancing around in her underwear telling you what you're both going to get up to and you're getting excited. Viagra's in the cupboard and you're sitting there with a bag of heroin. Talking about it. Dick's so hard, you didn't even notice what you said, did you?'

Harry had him.

'She's fucking dead,' he said. 'When this gets back to the bosses . . .'

'That's why I'm here. You see, I have my own deal for you.'

Zak's eyes narrowed. His lip curled. 'I'm listening.'

Harry leaned a little closer. 'You've broken parole. You've got four years left on your previous sentence. For this new charge, half a kilo of heroin, that's another four years. Puts you away for eight. I can live with that. Sure, *I* can't link the murders to you but I don't have to. Bradford-East knows you did it. Inside prison? You're a dead man. You think Bradford-West boys are going to protect you? Shit, you're nothing to them. A mid-level dealer, and now, a repeat offender. They will wash their hands.'

The reality dawned on Zak.

'You escape the life sentence for murder, but I don't see you getting out of jail.'

'How will they know it was me?' he asked, panic in his voice.

Harry stood up. 'I've been in these streets a long time. They ain't your streets, they're mine. All those high-up players in Bradford-West or Bradford-East, I know them all. We share intelligence. I'm going to drop your name to them.

100

When you go down, whether it's Armley or Wakefield, you will have a big, fat target on your back.'

Harry made to leave.

Zak got quickly to his feet, panicked. 'Wait, wait, I got information! Things I can trade!'

Gone was the big-time gangster. Zak was panicking.

Harry opened the door to leave. 'I don't do mid-level shit. Neither do my colleagues. This is Bradford. You fuckers are ten a penny. You're going to jail. And I would say it's fifty-fifty whether you come out alive.'

Chapter Twenty-two

Harry and Saima were at Mumtaz restaurant, one of the finest in Bradford. Saima was still convinced a spicy meal would start her labour. This was the third evening in a row road-testing the city's spiciest curries.

Saima ordered the hottest one on the menu. Harry opted for a couple of starters, not feeling particularly hungry.

'So now you've put your bad guy away, we can get back to finding a name for our baby girl.'

Harry smiled at his wife.

'Maria,' she said.

'Veto.'

'Why?'

'Sounds too religious. Makes me think of a church.'

'This baby is never going to have a name at this rate.'

'Harriet?' he tried.

'Harriet Virdee?'

'Like father, like daughter.'

'Veto. And I'm having Maria. It's going on the shortlist, nothing you can do about it.'

Harry watched as a stocky man in a turban entered the restaurant, his wife and daughter behind him.

The daughter. Deepi.

He had managed to keep her away from Saima at the wedding, but there was no way he could do that now.

'Shit,' muttered Harry to himself.

'What is it?' asked Saima.

'Nothing.'

She turned round to see the three of them waiting for a table.

'Who are they?' she asked Harry.

'Nobody.'

'Harry?' She leaned forward.

'He is Pardeep, head of the Sikh Society in Bradford. That's his wife and daughter.'

'How do you know them?'

'He's a friend of my father,' he said.

Saima wasn't stupid. 'Is that all?'

'Food's here,' said Harry, relieved to see the waiter.

Harry kept his head down, hoping Deepi and her family would just walk by.

'Well well well, if it isn't Hardeep Singh Virdee,' said Deepi.

Harry put on his best fake smile. 'Deepi and family. How lovely to see you all again.'

Deepi's father put his hand on her arm, muttered something and tried to move her away.

'You go ahead, Dad, I will catch up.'

Pardeep didn't move.

Deepi stared at Saima. 'You must be Mrs Virdee?'

'Yes. Saima.'

Deepi stuck out her hand.

Saima shook it. 'Pleased to meet you.'

Deepi leaned forward. 'Oh. As. Am. I.' Her tone was bitchy, although not quite threatening.

Harry glanced at Saima.

'We're in the middle of dinner, Deepi,' said Harry. 'Nice seeing you again.'

Deepi's father moved her on. They settled at the far end of the room.

Saima didn't touch her food. She just looked at Harry, waiting.

'She seemed nice.'

'Yeah.'

Harry could feel Saima's eyes on him.

'What was her name again?'

'Deepi.'

'You haven't mentioned her before.'

'Why would I?' Harry paused, his spoon of food hanging mid-air. 'Can't we just leave it?'

'I don't like the way she spoke to me. I would like to know why.'

104

'We dated.'

'When?'

'Before you.'

'I had hoped that was obvious. When, exactly?'

'Christ, I don't know. Eighteen months?'

'How long did you go out for?'

'About a year.'

'Did you sleep with her?'

Harry put his spoon down, fed up. He could see Deepi looking over, pleased with herself for causing a problem between him and Saima.

Saima started to slam food on to her plate. 'Bloody skinny ass, tight-suit-wearing slapper.'

Harry shook his head. His wife was as jealous a woman as he had ever known.

'And she had to see me like this. Fat. Sweaty. No make-up.'

Saima piled her food high, hammering the spoon on her plate with each helping.

'You're pregnant. Everyone can see that.'

'So, I do look fat?'

This wasn't an argument Harry was going to win.

'She better not come into A&E one day needing my help.'

Saima started to eat, still muttering to herself.

She had never dated anyone but him. And

Harry had never spoken of his past, knowing his wife got more than a little jealous.

'What about Amelia – that's a nice name,' said Harry, trying to change the subject.

'Eat your dinner,' she replied.

Harry reached for the naan.

'Don't choke on it, mind. I'm too fat to help you.'

Harry nearly spat his food out. He couldn't help but laugh.

'Are you kidding me?' she said, but he could see she was trying not to smile.

'Why do you get so jealous?'

'I don't. I'm ten times the woman she is.'

'Ten times heavier.'

She stopped eating, mouth open.

'Did you really just say that?'

Harry blew her a kiss.

Harry slipped some cash inside the small leather folder containing their bill and left it on the table. Deepi and her family had also finished and Harry was keen to leave before them.

He had managed to calm Saima down by agreeing that Maria was a name he could get on board with.

For now, at least.

Outside, he put his arm round Saima and

they crossed the road to the car park. Harry helped her into their car and was about to get in when he realized he had left his wallet on the table.

'Shit,' he whispered. 'One sec, Saima.'

Harry hurried back towards the restaurant. He saw Deepi outside, walking away towards the rear of the building.

'Thank fuck for that,' he muttered.

Inside, he got to his table, but his wallet wasn't there.

He grabbed a waiter. 'I left my wallet on there, just a few minutes ago. Has it been handed in?'

'No, sir. The gentleman sitting on that table' – the waiter pointed to where Deepi and her family had been sitting – 'said he knew you and would return it to you.'

'And you let him take it?' said Harry, amazed.

'Sir, I saw you speak when he came in. You don't know each other?'

Harry hurried outside.

At the back of the restaurant, Harry saw Deepi's father about to get into his car. Deepi and her mother were already inside.

'Hey!' said Harry, running towards him. 'My wallet?'

Pardeep chewed his lip and stood defiant.

'I don't have it.'

'The waiter just told me.'

'What waiter?'

'You need the money? Take it. It's been a while since I gave to charity.'

Harry regretted it as soon as he had said it.

Pardeep removed Harry's wallet and threw it on the floor.

Neither man moved.

Harry knew what Pardeep wanted. For him to crouch down so Pardeep could kick him. Harry simply folded his arms across his chest.

Deepi started to get out of the car, but Pardeep shouted to her to get back inside.

Pardeep stepped closer to Harry. 'At the wedding, you told my daughter that that pig you married had *everything*.'

Harry forced himself not to react. Calling Saima a pig was the worst of insults. The animal was considered dirty in Islam.

'Just get in your car and drive away. Nobody needs this.'

Pardeep spat on Harry's face.

Harry closed his eyes. He wiped his cheek with his sleeve.

'Your father should have killed you.'

Pardeep shoved Harry, hard, and spoke in Punjabi, a language in which insults could be delivered with more force than in English.

'If your pig was here, I would cut out the filth inside of her with my own knife.'

Rage took over. Before he knew what he had done, Harry's fist had connected with Pardeep's face.

The old man fell heavily to the ground.

Harry picked up his wallet as Pardeep rolled over, sat up and started to laugh.

The old man had got what he needed.

'I will have your job for this!' he yelled and laughed louder.

Harry walked away.

'You are a disgrace! You will never work as a police officer again!' shouted Pardeep after him.

Harry had assaulted a member of the public.

Once Pardeep filed his complaint, the only thing certain in Harry Virdee's future was suspension and an assault charge.

One way or another, Bradford had finally beaten him.

Acknowledgements

Thank you to retired detective Steve Snow for your continual support on the Harry Virdee series – it is invaluable!

I could not do this without the amazing input and hard work of Darcy Nicholson, Imogen Nelson and the team at Transworld.

To Jojo Moyes for rescuing the Quick Reads programme – a valuable and important scheme to support literacy – and for including me in this year's scheme.

To my agent, Simon Trewin, and the team at WME.

My inspiration these days comes from two little champions – my miniature Harry Virdees! You bring the sunshine on rainy days and I look forward to the time when you can read these books (aged eighteen and over!).

Final thanks as always to my wife for providing the best possible environment for me to create these stories. Always championing the series, looking after me and constantly inspiring me to continue. I'll finish with the same words I always write about you, Sam; keep doing what you do – it makes me do what I do.

Keep reading to find out what happens to Harry Virdee in

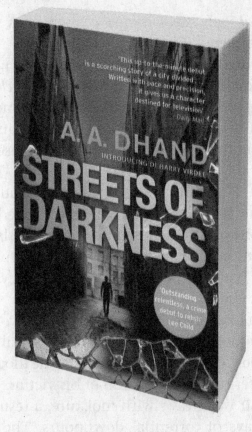

OUT NOW

Chapter One

Blood.

Arterial spray haemorrhaged across Harry's face.

He wondered if his karma was tainted.

When you accept a new life into the world, it will be without consequence as long as your karma is clean.

Perhaps it was because Saima was overdue. Or perhaps being suspended from duty meant he had more time to relive a past which refused to stay buried.

It was something the damn peer-saab had said to Saima the day before which was needling Harry. She had invited the holy man, an Islamic preacher who claimed he could predict the future, to their house to make sure her pregnancy was without issue.

Saima loved that shit.

Harry looked at his hands. He could still see the blood. You got away with murder, he thought, remembering the last scream of his victim.

The air was heavy with moisture, a result of three days of torrential downpours. The sun wouldn't cast its rays across Bradford – not unusual for October – but even in summer, it shied away, ensuring the bleakness that had strangled the city for over a decade remained firmly in place.

He ran harder through Lister Park, keeping off the grass which glistened with overnight dew. It was only five-thirty but Harry hadn't been able to sleep.

How could you be so reckless?

When he couldn't sleep, he ran, trying to tire his body into relenting. Harry preferred running in darkness: the park trapping shadows between the branches of hundreds of ageing oak trees. Saima thought it was dangerous. But Harry was six-three, ninety kilos of mostly muscle and spent his Sundays bulldozing rugby players as a second-row forward.

Harry slowed in front of the castellated gate-house at the north-east corner of the park and arrived at the Norman Arch exit. It had a medieval-looking gate. He placed his hands on it and rested his head against the iron. From the other side it might have appeared he was in jail. The image was fitting. Detective Inspector Harry Virdee suspended from work – IPCC investigation.

What a fucking joke.

His temperament was the problem. Always had been. Harry was tired of playing nice.

Especially in this city.

Especially with the choices he'd made.

Remember the blood, Harry? It's always about the blood.

He turned around and faced the hill which led up to the boating lake. He took a moment, glanced at the statue of Sir Titus Salt on his left and wondered what Bradford's most famous son would have made of the city now. In the 1800s, Titus had built the largest wool empire in Europe and made Bradford one of the richest cities in the world. Salt had created the entire suburb of Saltaire and built a village for his employees, complete with one of the most advanced wool mills ever seen.

Those times were gone. Bradford was a relic, its glory days past, suffocated by mass unemployment caused by the collapse of the textile industries. Salt's only legacy was a few books in the library and the dirty-white statue Harry was staring at. It had been moved from the entrance of the town hall to this corner of the park.

A forgotten legacy for a forgotten city.

Harry hit the incline hard, sprinting past Salt's statue. Grimacing against the pain, he blew out hot, stale air and tried not to close his eyes. He focused on the one memory which sat most uncomfortably in his mind. He recalled the wide-eyed horror of his victim and the flash of steel as Harry had hammered a pair of scissors into the man's neck.

The final image of his victim's eyes rolling lifelessly away before his body folded to the floor got Harry across the finish line.

Tonight Lister Park would be the setting for the start of the largest Asian Mela in England. The three-day event was returning after an absence of several years. Last year it had been in City Park in the town centre as a celebration of the new Centenary Square. There had been a live, televised stage show of *Bollywood Carmen*. It had been one of the largest-scale events to be held in the city.

This year Bradford Council had decided to return the event to Lister Park. They had good reason; today was also the Islamic festival of Eid and the turnout was going to be a record-breaker. Five thousand at least.

Harry was bringing Saima in the evening for some low-quality Asian food and to enjoy the bazaar-like atmosphere. She loved everything Asian.

Like Harry, Saima was trapped in a nightmarish world where she had crossed a religious divide by marrying outside of her faith. But whereas Harry had never been religious, Saima clung desperately to her Muslim identity. They had both been cast out by their families, an experience which was still raw. Harry was from an orthodox Sikh family and Saima from a strict Muslim household.

What had started as a taboo affair had evolved ultimately into a choice: their families or each other? Most days Harry reminded Saima that history was full of couples who had persevered, even when those close by disintegrated. She said she blamed him, his persistence in asking her out after a stint in A&E. Harry had split his head open during a scuffle with an assailant. Saima had stitched the wound and eventually agreed to dinner.

A few soft dates had turned into endless nights in bed, and finally an obsessive relationship had resulted in a marriage which cost them their families. Sikhs and Muslims were not supposed to mix. Harry routinely teased Saima that her bedside manner, whilst she had stitched his wound, was to blame. The pause which had held his eyes, the alluring scent of her skin, and the way she'd whispered seductively in his ear.

Harry trailed his feet against the gravel as he approached the exit, feeling the burn in his thighs subsiding. Saima didn't know Harry had been suspended. She was a week overdue with their first child and he didn't want to burden her. She would be tormented by worry about the consequences of Harry losing his job – money, stability and, moreover, what it meant for their future. It was on his mind too; Harry's head was bursting with questions he didn't have answers to. He realized how his file would read.

And this time?

This time, the IPCC would burn him.

He was a civilian, Harry. You nearly killed a civilian.

'Fuck,' he whispered.

A goddamn civilian.

Bastard deserved it. Sometimes the law didn't cut it. Son of a bitch is lucky I didn't . . .

The blood.

There it was again: surfacing in his mind like a clandestine tumour.

Harry clenched his fist and pressed it against his temple. His knuckle was sharp against the skin.

There's nothing you can do.

It wasn't true. There was one man who could have helped: Harry's father.

I'm not asking him. I'll die before I return there.

The Norman Arch took him out of the park on to Keighley Road, opposite Bradford Grammar, the most prestigious school in the city. It was a place Harry hoped his child might go to one day. But it would be impossible if he didn't have a job.

Saima was an A&E sister and, even if she went back to work full time, they wouldn't be able to afford an extravagance like private education. It was something Harry had experienced, and something he wanted to offer his own child.

He unlocked his ageing BMW – the black paint was smeared in dirt so thick it almost looked grey – but he didn't get in. The sight of a skulk of foxes running across the road into the grounds of the grammar school caught his attention. It wasn't especially uncommon at this early hour. The sun was yet to break and the roads were deserted. Commuter rush hour was at least two hours away. But there was something in the frenzied way they were moving – like a hunt.

Harry locked his car. He hadn't much else to do except make another bullshit excuse to Saima about why he wasn't at work. He crossed the road and climbed the shallow wall, into the enormous school grounds. Straight ahead was the main building.

The grass was treacherous to walk on. It hadn't been cut recently and was ankle high. His feet felt as though they were skating. It wasn't long before icy saturation worked through his trainers, soaked his socks and assaulted his toes.

Harry had tracked the foxes to a wide, triple-fronted sandstone building when the security lights came on. For a moment he stopped breathing.

The foxes were on their back legs, scrabbling up a wall, straining to get their teeth into a dangling pair of feet.

Harry let out his breath slowly. He clapped his hands together loudly and the animals ran, without turning to look at him.

Harry took tentative steps to his left so he was in front of the body. He focused on the wall.

The naked corpse of an older male was suspended, crudely crucified, three feet above the ground. There were rods through his outstretched wrists and his feet were not positioned traditionally but spread wide like da Vinci's Vitruvian Man.

Harry moved closer, mindful not to disturb the scene. He glanced behind and then to all four corners and was satisfied he was alone.

He crouched down and stared up at the face of the man. There wasn't enough light, so he took out his iPhone and turned on the torch. He held it high and, for a moment, couldn't quite believe his eyes.

There were words scrawled in blood on the wall next to the body: *Christ died for our sins; he died for his.*

But that wasn't the real cause of Harry's panic.

The man's identity was unmistakable. The most powerful Asian man in the city was staring lifelessly at him. There was a swastika brutally carved in the middle of his chest, blood still glistening.

Harry got to his feet and hurriedly dialled the third number in his recent call history.

Bradford, so often on the precipice, was suddenly primed to fall.

Chapter Two

Ninety minutes since Harry had discovered the body and Bradford Grammar was heaving with members of HMET, the Homicide and Major Enquiry Team. On any other day he'd be with them. Not today though: today he was an outcast. A witness at best.

His close colleagues were courteous, some engaging in banter. But others, the more senior members? They knew. They knew he was done. He wouldn't be returning to work.

He had been a boss they all looked up to, but a boss who, this time, had bent the rules so far they had boomeranged and returned to hit him on the arse.

It was half past seven when his own boss, Detective Superintendent George Simpson, arrived at the melee. He made his way past the SOCOs, detectives, forensics and uniforms to the hastily erected tent in front of the body. Harry hung back, away from the drama, spinning his mobile phone incessantly in his hands. It was excruciating not to be involved, not to be the senior investigating officer and organizing the scene. He was on the other side now and it felt like hostile territory. Awkward smiles, a few nods his way and plenty of questions from those who didn't know why he had been suspended. As they were discreetly updated, their mouths dropped open and they glanced clumsily his way.

Harry Virdee: story of the week.

But most of HMET were focused on the crime scene, because this was no ordinary murder.

Simpson spent half an hour checking details and liaising with officers before slowly making his way over to Harry, gait more laboured than usual, the cold stoking his arthritis.

George Simpson: five days from retirement with the mother of all crises on his hands. He looked forlorn and tired – more tired than Harry had ever witnessed. Simpson didn't just want retirement, he needed it. Bradford would do that to you.

He was cautious with his approach; the grass had already put three SOCOs on their backsides. Simpson's gold Rolex glimmered in the morning gloom as he drew nearer. 'Harry.'

'Sir.'

'Can't keep you out of mischief, can we?'

Harry shrugged.

'What were you doing out here at six-thirty?'

It wasn't an accusation. Just interest.

'Running,' replied Harry. 'Couldn't sleep. Not much else to do.'

Simpson nodded. It was awkward. The last conversation they'd shared had been heated, the suspension a foregone conclusion, the barrage of abuse he'd thrown at Harry warranted.

'You want to reinstate me? Help you clear this mess up?'

Simpson patted him on the shoulder. 'Let's walk a little, Harry. Away from here.'

They moved from the overloaded crime scene, back towards Lister Park. The sun had started its laboured ascent but the park was still sombre. The exterior of the Norman Arch had an obscenely yellow banner advertising the Mela, starting at eight o'clock that evening with a concert featuring 'Techno-Singh'. Pretty tacky and not really to Harry's taste, but the Mela would end on Sunday with a superb headline act: Feroz Khan, the world-renowned ghazal singer. He was a favourite of Harry's father, who would most certainly be attending. For that reason, much as he would have enjoyed it, Harry would be giving it a miss.

Their last meeting had drawn blood and Harry didn't want a repeat.

'There,' said Simpson, pointing past the statue of Sir Titus Salt. 'Up there.'

They headed up the hill where Harry had

finished his run. Now they were hidden from Bradford Grammar, Harry gently took hold of Simpson's arm and supported him up the steep incline. His boss was in the early stages of Parkinson's disease and Harry was one of only three senior officers who knew. Simpson didn't protest and they walked in an eerie silence past the boating lake towards Cartwright Hall into the Mughal Gardens.

'Like a different world, isn't it?' said Simpson, pointing at the flowers.

The garden had been designed to reflect the Asian cultural heritage of Bradford. Mughal architecture was a synergy between Islamic and Hindu designs and reflected the diverse ethnic mix of the city. A million pounds had been granted by the Heritage Lottery fund and the result was breathtaking.

There were beds of pink, red and yellow geraniums with a border of ferns protecting them. The flowers were guarded by a bronze statue of the Greek goddess of hunting, Diana. There was a natural tranquillity to the Mughal Gardens, usually complemented by the soft trickle of water from an adjacent fountain, which today had iced over.

'Agreed,' replied Harry. 'I'm always amazed this place hasn't been vandalized.'

'Always the cynic,' replied Simpson.

They were standing in the archway of Cart-wright Hall, in front of the flowers. Harry pointed back towards Bradford Grammar. 'Try telling that to Shakeel Ahmed.'

Simpson fell silent. Harry knew he was plagued by the violence in the city. Bradford was in the grip of an endemic drug problem which the police couldn't contain. It was now one of the most drug-fuelled cities in England with homicides on the rise.

'I'm not seeing things. Right? It was him?'

Simpson nodded. He scanned the entrance of the listed building and motioned for Harry to move away from the CCTV cameras, into the gardens, towards the water.

They walked past the statue of Diana and followed the path descending to a paved area. The fountain was dormant and the pond frozen.

'You want to tell me what this is about?' asked Harry.

Simpson pointed to a bench. An hour before, Harry had been sweating in the park but now the bitter chill was slicing through his clothing. They took a seat and Simpson turned towards Harry, his face tired and weary. 'Gotham City's on edge, Harry.'

'Jesus – not you as well?'

'It's true,' answered Simpson. 'I can't deny the comparisons any more.'

'That article was a joke. The only similarity between Gotham and Bradford is that we have a city full of dark knights and more than our fair share of jokers.'

Simpson grunted at the soft attempt at humour. 'PC as ever,' he replied. 'How I wish that were true.'

'You want to tell me how a guy who won the Bradford West by-election last night ended up crucified on that wall?'

Simpson took another cautious look around. But they were alone and well concealed from prying eyes.

'Ahmed was reported missing just after midnight. He left the victory party early; tired, we assume, from celebrating. When his son arrived at his father's residence he found signs of a break-in. Front door was smashed. Signs of a struggle in the kitchen.' He paused and then added: 'Blood.'

Shakeel Ahmed might not have been the new Titus Salt but he was a hugely influential businessman who had tried to reverse Bradford's decline. In the city's heyday the population had dramatically increased, with hundreds of textile mills providing thousands of jobs. That industry was now dead. The factories were closed. The city's fortunes had taken an unprecedented fall and unemployment was at a record high. Thousands of immigrants, welcomed into Bradford to work in the sixties, had found themselves without prospects when the trade collapsed, unable to educate themselves or find alternative jobs. Bradford crumbled into a bleakness from which it couldn't recover.

Ahmed was a first-generation immigrant who had left the textile mills and started a small takeaway. Now, it was a chain of eleven restaurants. 'Ahmed's' routinely won Bradford's 'Indian restaurant of the year', which was no mean feat – there were hundreds of them in the city. Ahmed had also been given a MBE in 2008 for services to Yorkshire. He had built three mosques, owned several charitable foundations and had recently funded a new wing at Bradford Royal Infirmary.

'How long before Forensics get any data? Have we ruled out the son?'

Simpson ran a wrinkled hand through grey hair and sighed. His watch sparkled again before disappearing beneath his raincoat.

'You already know who it is, don't you?' said Harry, leaning closer to his boss.

'Yes,' he replied.

There was something troubling Simpson. He was hesitating, grimacing at the question he knew was coming next.

129

'Who?'

'Before I answer, Harry, I need something from you,' replied Simpson.

'I'm listening.' Harry's breath formed a white mist in the air.

'I need your assistance.'

'Can you help me with next week?' replied Harry, almost too eagerly.

Simpson shook his head. 'What happened is on you, Harry, and you alone. There isn't a damn thing I can do.' He paused and then added, 'There is, however, something you can do to "help" your case.'

'I'm all ears.'

'I need you to operate off the books on this one. You're in enough trouble as it is, so I'll understand if you refuse.'

'I'm not sure what you're—'

'You will.' Simpson held out his hand to silence Harry. 'In all the years I've known you, I've never asked you how you solved so many cases. Nobody has your success rate.'

Harry felt an unease prickling through his body. Simpson's tone was tinged with ambiguity.

'But I also know . . .' He paused, poking Harry gently in the chest and waiting until he met his gaze. '. . . that no one achieves those kinds of results without *help*.'

'Meaning?' Harry blurted out before he could stop. He didn't want to pursue this conversation.

'Meaning that I've always taken a back seat when it came to exploring where or how you got your information. You seem to have every convict in Bradford in your pocket and I don't know how you've managed it. Truth be told, I never much cared because as long as the cases were brought to a satisfactory conclusion, my job was done.'

'I keep my ear to the ground,' said Harry. 'That's all.'

'No, Harry. We all do that. Hell, I've got detectives with twenty years more experience and far more brains who can't deliver what you do.'

'They don't work hard enough.'

Simpson shook his head. 'That's not fair, Harry. They work hard. But no one works like you. No one needs to. You punish yourself. It's the perpetual need to prove something. Look, we're getting off the point here.'

A couple of blackbirds hopped on to the fountain. They lowered their beaks cautiously to the surface.

'Hardeep—'

'Harry,' he corrected. 'I'm not in trouble. Why don't you just cut to the chase, sir? What *is it* that you want?'

'I need your help. Off the books. You know the streets better than anyone. I need you to find Shakeel Ahmed's killer.'

'And that is who exactly?'

'First I need your word this won't go—'

'Jesus,' said Harry impatiently. 'As if you even have to say it?'

'I do. Right now, I need to hear it. Because when I tell you what I know – you'll understand. I need to contain this for as long as I can. So I need your utmost discretion.'

'You have it,' replied Harry. 'In spite of my current predicament, you still have my loyalty. So, who am I tracking?'

'I'm asking you because you seem to enjoy working outside the constraints of the law which the rest of us abide by. And today I'm asking you to do whatever it takes to find me Lucas Dwight.'

Harry stared at Simpson, momentarily lost for words. The blackbirds stopped pecking at the ice and fixed their jet-black eyes on the men.

'What?' whispered Harry, as if saying the name out loud might trigger a curse.

'His DNA was found at Shakeel Ahmed's house. We got a match a few hours ago,' said Simpson.

'He's – he's . . . in jail?'

'No,' replied Simpson solemnly, 'he's not. He was released four days ago.'

The Harry Virdee series

About Quick Reads

*"Reading is such an important
building block for success"*
- Jojo Moyes

Quick Reads are short books written by
best-selling authors. They are perfect for regular
readers and adults reading for pleasure for
the first time. Since 2006, over 4.8 million copies
of more than 100 titles have been read!

Available to buy in paperback or ebook and to
borrow from your local library.

Turn over to find your next Quick Read...

A special thank you to Jojo Moyes
for her generous donation and support of Quick Reads
and to **Here Design**.

Quick Reads is part of The Reading Agency, a national
charity tackling life's big challenges through
the proven power of reading.
www.readingagency.org.uk
@readingagency   #QuickReads

The Reading Agency Ltd. Registered number: 3904882 (England & Wales)
Registered charity number: 1085443 (England & Wales)
Registered Office: Free Word Centre, 60 Farringdon Road, London, EC1R 3GA
The Reading Agency is supported using public funding by Arts Council England.

Supported using public funding by
**ARTS COUNCIL
ENGLAND**

Find your next Quick Read:
the 2020 series

More from Quick Reads

For a complete list of titles and more information
on the authors and stories visit

www.readingagency.org.uk/quickreads

THE
READING
AGENCY

Quick
Reads

Continue your reading journey

The Reading Agency is here to help keep you
and your family reading:

Challenge yourself to complete six reads
by taking part in **Reading Ahead**
at your local library, college or workplace
readingahead.org.uk

Join **Reading Groups for Everyone** to find a
reading group and discover new books
readinggroups.org.uk

Celebrate reading on **World Book Night**
every year on 23 April
worldbooknight.org

Read with your family as part of the
Summer Reading Challenge
at your local library
summerreadingchallenge.org.uk

For more information, please visit our website:
readingagency.org.uk